The Letter of Alon

By J.S. Knox

RESOURCE *Publications* • Eugene, Oregon

Resource Publications
A division of Wipf and Stock Publishers
199 W 8th Ave, Suite 3
Eugene, OR 97401

The Letter of Alon
By Knox, John S.
Copyright©2013 by Knox, John S.
ISBN 13: 978-1-5326-9315-1
Publication date 5/31/2019
Previously published by Crosslink Publishing, 2013

Contents

To Jacob and Joseph.

May you keep Psalm 139 close to your hearts

as you add your own chapters

to the story of faith.

Foreword

The search for God is nearly as old as humanity itself, and the discussion of faith and reason has always followed closely behind. Famously, St. Anselm of Canterbury, in one of his theological proofs, offered two facets of the human person: faith seeking reason (*fides quaerens intellectum*) as two complimentary ways to live more fully in God. Unfortunately, our culture continues to divide faith and reason into opposing camps. Popular literature is also guilty of this approach; however, *The Letter of Alon* nobly takes license to bring the modern reader into the biblical world wherein familiar characters come into new light. It engages the reader to think with his or her imagination, all the while building up the faith. It unabashedly brings faith and reason back together in a work of fiction so that the reader can better grasp the mysteries of God in history.

We all suffer from various trials in our lives. We all seek out explanations for events that sometimes are simply beyond us to comprehend. Sadly, the media and secular presentations that surround us all too often can (and do) lead us to fallacious conclusions or to no hope, whatsoever. Fortunately, faith-based fiction, such as Dr. John S. Knox offers in his current work, *The Letter of Alon*, adds to the growing work of Christian writers who desire to promote and encourage a faith of reason, and to remind believers of the foundations of their hope. By setting his story in a Christian milieu, the author not only reminds us of the normative place faith plays in so many lives, but also how important faith is when crises come. He creatively crafts his story around biblical characters (which brings intrigue to his work) as well as references to the canonical texts, which we love so dear. He reminds us that God continues to be active in our world and that nobody is beyond salvation.

I applaud Dr. Knox for his tireless work as a teacher of history and Christian theology in expanding the minds of his students, but even more so for his desire to reinfuse, dare I say, the evangelization of our culture, so as to remember the ageless truths about Jesus that were handed down to us through Sacred Revelation and Church tradition. A new evangelization has begun, and our culture and time needs to grasp the Gospel now more than ever. Dr. Knox engages the reader with a story of crisis and redemption. He stimulates the mind and stirs our imaginations of life to help us grow in faith.

May the hearts of all who read *The Letter of Alon* come to know the gift of God, which ultimately is Love.

Rev. William Holtzinger
St. Anne Church
Grants Pass, Oregon

Acknowledgements

Blaise Pascal wrote, "Faith is different from proof; the latter is human, the former is a Gift from God." His words reverberate in my heart, and I truly am appreciative for the unexpected opportunities afforded me in life by Him who gives me salvation and purpose for living—this book being a small joyful facet of my life's journey.

Thus, I would like to thank all the people who have made this book possible.

First, eternal gratitude to my wife and family—Brenda and Jacob and Joseph—for their unconditional love, patience, and support in my journey to be used by God. Sincerely, it has been so easy to imagine and illustrate the good in my literary characters, for I have firsthand experience of it from them. I am blessed.

Second, I owe much to my former professors for sharing with me their knowledge, wisdom, and craft(s). Dr. Gary Ferngren first lit the fire of historical inquiry in my mind as a freshman at OSU. Dr. Dan Brunner and Dr. Carole Spencer provided the fuel for deeper historical studies in my graduate studies at GFU. Dr. Ben Dandelion helped me refine the scholarly skills of truthfulness and intellectual honesty in my PhD pursuit, and Dr. Chris Anderson showed me more artful ways to express timeless and time-full truths as a post-bacc (finishing up a BA in English at OSU, which I began twenty-eight years ago). These men and woman helped me be a better person, although in all ways I am still learning what it means to be a good teacher, historian, theologian, and writer. Truly, I hope my lessons never end.

Third, a warm and hearty thank you is required for George Fox student Heather Harney for kindly and enthusiastically being the first reader of *The Letter of Alon* as I fumbled through the initial drafts of my novel. Always honoring, she provided honest feedback and beneficial input with each chapter to the end. She is a star.

Finally, I must thank God the Father in heaven for his wonderful and majestic plans for my life. I never could have dreamed to do the things He has enabled and empowered me to do in life. This book, my writing, my teaching, my involvement in being part of something so much bigger and grander than mere existence have been a constant source of joy and hope in living. I only wish others could join with me in following Mother Teresa's advice for life:

> "Life is an opportunity, benefit from it. Life is beauty, admire it. Life is a dream, realize it. Life is a challenge, meet it. Life is a duty, complete it. Life is a game, play it. Life is a promise, fulfill it. Life is sorrow, overcome it. Life is a song, sing it. Life

is a struggle. accept it. Life is a tragedy, confront it. Life is an adventure. dare it. Life is luck, make it. Life is too precious, do not destroy it. Life is life. fight for it."

Thank you one and all! ~ JSK

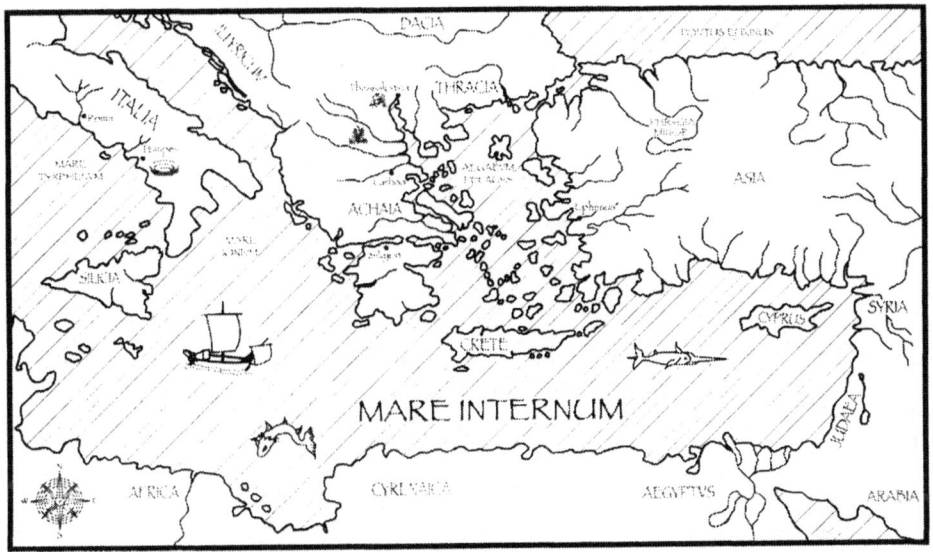

The World of Alon in AD 75

Prologue

"A farmer went out to sow his seed. As he was scattering the seed, some fell along the path, and the birds came and ate it up. Some fell on rocky places, where it did not have much soil. It sprang up quickly, because the soil was shallow. But when the sun came up, the plants were scorched, and they withered because they had no root. Other seed fell among thorns, which grew up and choked the plants. Still other seed fell on good soil, where it produced a crop—a hundred, sixty or thirty times what was sown. Whoever has ears, let them hear." ~ Luke 8

Eldad saw the bearded man step out of the Galilean synagogue, with a mob of people following him closely. Some in the crowd were smiling; others looked mad as Hades; still others had bewildered expressions. The man was plainly dressed, but walked as if he had to be at an important meeting. Every few steps, the man would stop to talk to a person, normally weeping. Eldad saw him place his hands on their heads time and time again before moving on—he wasn't able to travel very fast through town.

A young woman came out of the synagogue and sat down on the marbled steps leading up to the giant bronze doors of the house of worship. Eldad made his way toward her, careful to not draw attention to himself and his condition. As he came within steps of the woman, he pulled his cloak further over his head.

Standing beside her without looking directly at her, Eldad said, "What's all this craziness about?"

The woman stared down at her hands and replied, "He's the healer from the countryside."

"Another liar selling hope," Eldad blurted out, shaking his head. "People flock to these men like flies to dung, and for what? Ten minutes of false emotion followed by years of disappointment."

"You're wrong," the woman said, raising her teary eyes to look at Eldad. "His gift is real."

He laughed and said, "How do you know for certain?"

The woman looked up into the sky and said, "Because. . . he healed me." Tears began to run down her face. She held up her left hand and said, "Look! My hand was crushed when I was just a child."

Eldad responded, "Wha—? You lie."

The woman jumped up and nearly yelled to him. "He healed my broken, useless hand! Ask anyone around the marketplace about me— they all know me well. Yiskah the Cripple. Yiskah the Sad and Lonely, but look! Look!" She held up her hand in front of his face, and, true enough, it looked perfect to Eldad. So beautiful, it almost seemed to glow in the morning Sabbath sunlight.

"It can't be," he said. "No one does miracles anymore."

She grabbed him by the shoulders and said, "He is the Messiah!" But her words were lost in Eldad's horror as his cloak fell down by his side, uncovering the leprous sores and disfigurement of his face. He heard her let out a gasp and he knew why. One ear was gone as was most of his nose, and his left eye had clouded over, giving him a corpse-like appearance. He felt the blood drain from his face, and coldness cover his body.

Instinctively, he raised his arms to protect his head and curled his body down low. He knew how people treated his kind, especially when they sneak into town and pretend to be part of the community of God, pretend to be human again, even for a short time. Soon, the screams of terror would come, followed by the taunts, and then the rocks. Rocks and kicks and pain. He prayed that it wouldn't be as vicious as last time.

He closed his eyes and waited for the assault to begin, but instead, he felt the woman firmly grab under his arm and pull him toward the crowd down the street. "Come with me," she commanded. He consigned himself to his presumed fate by the mob. He was surprised at how strong she was. Perhaps he was just very weak.

"Where is he?" the woman cried out. Not letting go of Eldad, she asked one of the stragglers, "The healer, where did he go?" The man pointed to his right and then pulled back in revulsion when he noticed her companion. Peering carefully over the mass of people in the street, she saw the healer duck into a narrow corridor, and she followed him in, dragging Eldad along with her. She called out, "Wait! Oh, someone make him wait." Desperately, she called out, "Yeshua! Stop!" and the man stopped and turned around. She pushed her way through the crowd, holding on tightly to Eldad's arm, until they both stood in front of the healer. "Help him. Please?"

Eldad's eyes darted about, wide and terrified, like a sheep caught in a briar, looking for an escape, any route away from his impending doom. He didn't dare to look into the eyes of the bearded man he had seen come out of the assembly. He fell to his knees at the healer's feet, head down, and begged him, "Help me, Master. If you can, make me clean again."

The healer said nothing, and, with the last courage he could find, Eldad raised his ugly face to receive the sentence of his judge. What he saw in the healer's face surprised him—not anger, not disgust, not pity. He saw only emotional embrace with a touch of *you-don't-think-I-can-do-it?* in Yeshua's eyes.

With Eldad still kneeling before him, Yeshua placed both his hands on either side of Eldad's scarred, disfigured cheeks, and said to him, "I am willing, Eldad." The healer began to talk to Yahweh as if He were standing there with them.

Eldad's immediate confusion of how the man could know him by name was washed away by the wave of intense power he felt coming from the healer's hands, coursing through his sick body. But it wasn't fiery hot—it was comforting and tingled, like when his mom used to scratch his back under his tunic as a boy sitting by the evening fire before he became a monster and she abandoned him up to God's apparent curse. This sensation didn't burn him, though. This soothed. He closed his eyes and felt a tranquility he had never before experienced. He felt the pain leave him like dust washing off his body in a warm summer rain.

Eventually, the healer let go of Eldad's face and told him, "Rise. Don't tell this to anyone, but immediately go to the synagogue and show yourself to the priest there. Offer the proper sacrifices that Moses commanded as your testimony to all. Do that first, Eldad." Eldad could only look at the man; he didn't know what to say.

He gazed at Eldad, kindly, almost playfully, and then tweaked his nose before walking off. Eldad stayed on his knees, realizing he had just felt his nose for the first time in five years, and it didn't hurt. Hands trembling, he slowly reached up and felt warm smooth skin on his cheeks. He touched more of his face and discovered he had nostrils! Nostrils! And, yes, he had his ear back, too.

"Let me see," his female guide commanded.

She lifted his chin up and turned his head side-to-side, smiling. "Beautiful." Their eyes met and she said, "I told you."

He stood up and took her hand, the first woman's hand he had touched since he became an untouchable, and said, "Thank you. . . "

"Yiskah," she replied, "but don't thank me. Thank God."

"I thank you both." He wanted to hug her, but held back; he did continue to hold her hand, however, and she didn't object at all.

The two began to walk back toward the synagogue. Eldad remembered what the healer had asked him to do, but their pace grew quicker and quicker as they began to think about whom they were going to share the good news with. Soon, they were stopping to tell everyone they could about this healer of Nazareth who had changed their lives forever.

Chapter One

Discovery

The old red oak door swung open, its squeak testifying to how long the upstairs attic room had been abandoned. The shaft of light from the hallway cut through the dusty air, and William Berrit peered inside, coughing a bit from the stale air; yet his eyes grew wide with interest as he looked at the collection of chairs, lamps, and boxes strewn about the crypt-like room. He felt like Carter discovering the long-lost treasure of the boy-king forgotten for ages. He fumbled for the light switch, and a solitary hanging bulb flickered on, illuminating the darkness and mystery.

William moved to the middle of the attic, stooping slightly, lest his head bang on the rafters and roof above. He noticed a dark, oily rag covering what appeared to be the impression of an old window on the far wall. Walking to it, his footsteps caused the floor below to creak, and he hoped he wouldn't fall through the aged wood. His Uncle Les hadn't been able to take care of the century-old house for some time, and the wear and tear of life slowly dimmed the beauty and strength of this family dwelling, which William and his brother Matt had inherited after his uncle's death.

He pulled down the dirty towel from the window, and more light filled the small room. William looked around and pondered how he was going to go through all this memorabilia and mementos of the family. He recognized some of the possessions from his childhood, but behind them were boxes and boxes of unknown origin and contents.

Matt bounded up the stairs and called out to his brother. "Tell me you found some old Chevron or Apple stocks, and that we are now part of the nouveau riche!"

William smiled because he hoped the same thing. "Nope. I think we are still stuck with that Hindenburg stock great-grandpa bought before WWII."

Matt held up an o,d clock-radio topped with what appeared to be a tarnished, bronzed sports trophy adorned with velvet and streamers. "Think we can get anything for this?" he asked.

William replied, "Maybe tetanus."

"This is going to take a long time to go through," Matt muttered. "Good thing you're used to boring research!"

William knew where this was headed. "Now wait a minute, bro. We both inherited the house. You have to help, too."

Matt slapped his brother on the shoulder and said, "I will, I will, but you are better at this sorting stuff than I am. I'll deal with the repairs and potential demolition," he said smiling, "and you deal with the financial stuff."

William clenched his teeth and managed to reply, "Okay, Matthew, but I might just pocket any gold jewelry I find, and you'll be sorry."

On his way out, Matt paused at the top of the stairs and said, "That's the one thing I know I don't have to worry about, dear brother. You and I both know that you're horrible at keeping secrets. Besides, you love me."

William picked up an old beach ball and threw it at Matt. "Out, prodigal child!" The ball hit Matt in the back of the head, and he pretended to fall down the stairs.

With his brotherly distraction gone, William turned his attention to the project at hand. The easiest thing to do would be to kick out the little window and toss the boxes, furniture, and knickknacks into a dumpster below. However, this attic didn't just hold the former belongings of Uncle Les (who was slightly nuts); this house was also the home for their grandparents and even great-grandparents. William felt a sense of moral obligation to go through the stacks of boxes to honor the family heritage. Plus, Matt was right about him being good at sorting through the attic's ancient contents—he was the history professor, the "history geek" as Matt called him, and he might be able to better understand the value of an item not covered in gold or jewels.

In his typical systematic fashion, William began his exploration of the room's belongings. As for the larger items, he discovered that the attic contained six wooden chairs, a few of them probably made before 1900, a Singer Sewing Machine with carrying case, two rusty tricycles, a small metal cabinet painted pink, a hula hoop, a bedside table, the front grill of an old Ford truck (he had no idea why that would be in the attic), two vacuum cleaners clearly never used in this room, a broken futon, several stacks of family board games purchased before the advent of computers, several framed portraits leaning together of people William did not know—a few of them faced each other and he wondered if the subjects were married—and an assortment of old rolled up rugs.

Toward the back of the attic, the boxes began to have very dated material in them from before WWII. Even the boxes themselves smelled old, like walking through an antiques shop or a musty museum. William got excited when he discovered a stash of textbooks from the 1920s. He yelled down and alerted Matt regarding the book prize, who responded with a loud, obnoxious yawn and a request to "Please leave the kingdom of boredom which is this house." William didn't care, though, because the books had given him hope that this room might hold more treasures. With increasing fascination, he dug through the boxes, and, sure enough, he found more vintage objects from the decades before, but nothing to get too excited about, until he got to the last row.

Pulling one of the last boxes to him, he saw a flash of light in the darkness of the far corner of the attic. William muttered, "Hello, there. What's this?" Moving the other box aside, the attic bulb illuminated a small metallic chest with no markings on it. It looked handmade and archaic, much older than a century.

Matt poked his head into the room and said, "Bro, I am done for the night. Do you know that you've been up here for three hours?"

William turned to Matt and said, "I think I found a chest here. Looks really old."

Matt rolled his eyes and replied, "Ooh, how exciting! Have fun with that. Ciao, bro." And with that, Matt bounded out as quickly as he had come into the attic.

William thought for a moment of going after his brother, but he really didn't know what was in the chest. It could just be some antediluvian Tupperware or it could be empty, but he knew he had to check it out. He and Matt had joked earlier about finding treasure, but William somehow sensed this might just be that. His heart beating faster, he reached for the chest and wondered what lay within.

The chest itself was about one foot high and deep and about a foot and a half wide. He grabbed the chest by the leather handles on either side and had to pull hard a couple of times, as it was stuck to the floor, having sat in the same place for several decades. It was heavier than he expected, and William moved the chest beneath the hanging attic bulb with a grunt.

There was a lock and clasp to the chest, but it wasn't fastened. Kneeling in front of it, William slowly opened the chest and peered inside. It only held two items—a small inscribed brass crucifix resting on top, and what looked like a book wrapped in an oil rag with a thin cord holding it together at the bottom. William picked up the cross and examined it closely. It wasn't anything fancy, but it had some Greek words scratched into it that William once knew. The cross looked old and weathered, like it had been used much in its day. He carefully set it down and pulled out the wrapped book, closing the lid of the chest.

Placing the bundle upon the chest, he untied the cord, folded back the cloth wrap, and stared down at what appeared to be a very ancient book at least six inches thick. At first, William thought it was a Bible, but when he opened it up to the front page, he saw English handwriting, which said, "The Faith of our Family." William turned to the next yellowed page and began to read what seemed to be a letter. It stated:

"Dear Son or Daughter of God,

I, Reverend Alexander Joseph Berrit, pastor of the New Haven Congregational Church, have been entrusted with this Epistle and family crucifix passed down from generation to generation since the beginnings of the early church. My grandfather, Rev. Lemuel P. Berrit, also pastor of the New Haven Congregational Church, gave it to me in the year 1820 before his passing (God rest his soul), and his grandfather, Anglican Bishop Cecil T. Berrit, passed it on to him in 1750, and so on, back unto the founding of our faith. The original documents were written in Latin, which my grandfather graciously translated and compiled in this tome, and those early documents rest with him in his grace in Westminster Abbey, London.

This is not just a mere storybook; it is a treasure that links past and present believers in heart and soul and purpose. Few people know not how they landed upon the path of righteousness. This letter introduces the Berrit family lineage and heritage in communion with the Lord God through his Son, Jesus Christ, throughout the past twenty centuries until the present day.

May God open your eyes to the great sacrifice and devotion of your ancestors described within, who, through great love and devotion, fought the good fight and brought the blessings of God to all generations of his humble servants.

God bless and keep you all until His glorious return.

With the utmost of Sincerity and Hope,
Alexander J. Berrit, DD
August 29, 1856

William closed the book, stood up, and quickly moved out of the attic to the kitchen of Uncle Les's house. He poured himself a cold Pepsi out of the refrigerator before sitting down at the maple dining table in the middle of room with the book. He turned to the first letter entry entitled, "Catacombs," and began to read the first transcription of his great-grandfather.

Chapter Two

Catacombs

The first letter entry began with, "Praise the Almighty for the blessings bestowed up the descendants of Alon Beryit and his daughter, Naamah, who entered into the holy community of Jesus Christ, the Messiah, Son of God, and Savior of the world in the year of our Lord, A.D. 45, and began the golden tapestry of faith that has been woven together through the family stories that follow them. Their journey was not an easy one, but they fought the good fight and found the prize."

Naamah walked down the main street of Larissa, holding her father's hand as they made their way toward old town. The constant wind from nearby mountains stirred up dust in the road, so that the street vendors appeared like ghosts in the smoky, brownish-orange haze. The sellers and buyers seemed to be in a yelling contest, and Naamah drew closer to her father, trying to put as much distance as possible between her and the angry people.

Neither of them was smiling; in fact, one could hardly tell that they were on their way to celebrate anyone's birthday. But who could blame them? It had been just three days since Eldad had been murdered—pulled from his home by a bloodthirsty mob, stirred up by the local oracle who blamed the plague on the missionary and his new movement that angered the Gods. What else could it be?

Eldad did not resist them, nor did he fight back when they began to beat him mercilessly. To his last breath, he kept praying for them, crying out what he remembered the Master saying, which only angered them more. Again and again, he said, "Father, forgive them," and "Today you will be in paradise." The crowd hissed at him like vicious vipers getting ready to lunge.

From the shadows of a nearby doorway, Naamah's father, Alon, had seen the horde throw stones at the poor gentleman, until blood ran like a river from his head and his heart gave out. Worried that he, too, would be murdered by this frenzied pack of wolves, Alon stole back to the safety of his home to tearfully tell his family about what had happened. The loss was devastating to the whole community of believers, and it felt unbearable. Why had God allowed this to happen?

Alon and Naamah approached the entrance to the city cemetery. As he swung open the rusty gate to enter the graveyard, he glanced around. The street seemed empty; few people wanted to visit such a morbid location. They slipped through the gravestones and chalky tombs to the back of the necropolis, and then entered a small marble vault.

The chamber itself was unassuming, with plain walls, no windows, and one modest sarcophagus near the back of the room; but its looks were deceiving. The crypt contained a well-hidden passageway leading down to the ancient catacombs that lay underneath the city. A small oil lamp burned on the sarcophagus. Alon picked up a small candle from a box lying on the ground near the opening, lit it, and then, holding Naamah's hand, moved into the catacombs. He said to her, "Stay close."

Naamah was surprised at the smell of the underground passage. The earthiness was there, yes, but the faint odor of incense and perfume also wafted from the wall niches containing the dead. It didn't take them long to move through the maze of alcoves before they came to a dimly lit room occupied by several people—three men, two women, and another child.

Alon let go of Naamah's hand and rushed to the eldest man in the group, and they embraced. Naamah heard her father weep into the old man's shoulder, and she saw the man pat her father on the shoulder. It troubled her to see her father so sad.

"Courage, Alon. This is not the end; it is only the beginning," he said.

Alon responded, "I. . . know, Barnabas. It's just that he was the one who first told me about Yeshua." Barnabas kept Alon at arm's length and said, "Yes, Eldad was an amazing man who shared the love of the

Moshiach with all he could. Truly, Yeshua would have been proud of him. . . and you, my friend."

"I'm not sure about that," Alon said, wiping tears from his eyes.

"Believe it, brother." Barnabas walked to a center table in the room with one big bright candle on it and said, "Eldad wouldn't want us to wallow in sorrow for him, because he's now with the Son, in unimaginable joy and comfort, as we all will be, eventually."

"Like Mama," Naamah interjected.

"Yes, child, like your mother," Barnabas replied.

One of them said, "Amen," and others quickly echoed her.

"Violent men are filled with darkness because their gods are false; they have no hope; they have nothing to soothe the pain in their hearts. But we do. Yeshua taught us what love really means and from where true hope rises, like the water from a spring that no one can stop."

Barnabas picked up the candle from the table and moved to the wall behind him, which was covered with unlit candles.

"They try to snuff us out, but they can never put out the light of God." Barnabas held up the candle above his head. "And this light is shared by the Holy Family—Father, Son, and Holy Sprit." He lit two candles near the top of the wall. "God's light illuminates the hearts and minds of all who embrace it." He lit three more candles underneath the top two.

"Even though some die for the faith. . ." he said, lighting two red candles under the five. "Even though some pass over more peacefully. . ." he said, lighting two white candles beside the red ones, ". . . the love of God shines ever brighter with each believer who lovingly shares it with his brother and sister."

Soon, all the candles were lit on the wall—a mixture of red and white luminescence. Finally, he placed the white candle at the top of the wall. The light cascaded down it and the whole room was filled with the candles' radiance.

"So, as we celebrate the birth of the Savior, Yeshua, this winter morning, let's not forget what was spoken to the shepherds in the fields long ago. *Do not be afraid. I bring you good news of great joy that will be for all the people. Today in the town of David a Savior has been born to you; he is Christ the Lord.*"

They all began to sing a hymn, and Naamah felt the warmth of the candles on her face and in her heart. For Alon, though, it was a bittersweet moment. He wanted to feel the hope of Barnabas and his five-year-old daughter, but it seemed so unfair to him that good, loving people, like his wife and Eldad, died because of their kindness and mercy. God should reward that—not allow it to be cruelly snuffed out. Alon saw the candlelights; he felt their warmth, but he felt cold inside. And his heart ached for release.

Chapter Three

The Road to Sikyon

Gaius and Aelia followed behind the rickety ox cart in front of them as they walked toward Sikyon, a small town about ten miles from Corinth. They were traveling to visit with her parents—pottery makers. And as much as Gaius enjoyed spending time with Aelia's kind parents, the trip from cosmopolitan Corinth to rural Sikyon was always a long, dirty, smelly one. This Roman road was good and straight, but even with the gutters to carry waste (both human and beast), both had to look with care to where they put their feet down. The trip would take nearly all day, and Gaius was impatient for it to be over already.

Having grown up in the fertile hills that surrounded Sikyon, Aelia hardly noticed the earthy sights and smells that surrounded them on their journey. She was excited to visit her mater and pater—Ma and Pa—to inform them that she and Gaius were expecting their first child, which would be her parents' first grandchild, a glorious event long prayed for. The news would be welcomed loudly and in lengthy fashion. Her parents knew how to celebrate well, even Gaius would agree.

In her third month, Aelia was just showing and her morning nausea had ceased. The whole idea of carrying a baby inside her was still somewhat unreal, but already she felt emotions she had never experienced before—she was both joyful and terrified, and the feelings switched prominence without a moment's notice sometimes. She hoped she wasn't being too difficult for Gaius.

Tiring of following behind the smelly, noisy cart, Gaius took her arm and the reins of their mule, Tiberius, and applied some speed to move them in front of the lumbering beast at a choice crossroad location. "Ave," Gaius said to the old man on the cart. Without looking at them, the man responded, "Avete."

His stoicism was unpleasant to Aelia but not unfamiliar. Lately, she had felt that the people of Corinth and many of its surrounding communities were growing colder and colder. She remembered when people seemed happy to greet each other, and strangers would break out in conversations, but that was before Corinth became so busy and rich. People were no longer as important as profit, and Aelia wondered what world her child would inherit from them.

Her annoyance with the old man was interrupted, though, by the desperate cries of a nearby baby. Her motherly instincts kicked into high gear as she recognized that the baby's sounds were due to fear rather than hunger. Her eyes scanned the busy road for the baby, but didn't see it in the arms of any of their fellow journeyers. It was then that she saw the baby lying in a wood basket by the side of the road, no parent in sight. In fact, most people were going out of their way to avoid the child. Aelia, however, made a beeline for the baby.

Gaius saw what she was doing and said firmly, "Aelia, no." Ignoring him, she bent down and picked up the baby, which was wrapped in tattered, dirty clothing. She rewrapped the child so that it was better covered and noticed that it was a girl. "Poor little thing," Aelia said soothingly, as she pulled the baby girl close to her.

Trying to show some restraint and patience, considering her condition, Gaius spoke to his wife, "We will be lucky to afford our own child, let alone adding another mouth to feed. Besides, we have no need of a servant yet. Maybe in a few years, once my business is grown."

Rocking the baby side to side, Aelia cooed and shushed, until the child's cries lessened. "This baby needs food, Gaius, or she will die."

Fists on his hips, he responded, "Aelia, we're not taking it."

"Her," Aelia corrected him.

"Whatever," Gaius replied.

Reaching out for the baby, he said, "You know we can't do this right now." Aelia protectively pulled the baby close to her but knew Gaius wouldn't let her keep the child. His hands remained outstretched. She started to cry and handed the baby over to him. He carefully put the child back into the wood crate. "Maybe the gods will find someone for her, Aelia." Saying nothing, she turned her face away from him, weeping, and walked away from the baby girl. Aelia's sorrow felt heavier than a cart of bricks, but there was nothing she could do. Gaius wasn't a mean man, but he was ruthlessly practical. Perhaps it was part of his personality or perhaps it was the consequence of being an auxiliary soldier in the Roman army some years before they married.

Gaius caught up with her and put his arm around her lovingly. He appreciated his wife's compassion—it was one of the things about her that attracted him initially—but life was difficult for everyone, and people had to look out for themselves first to survive. That child was none of their business and could hurt their financial status. As they continued their walk toward Sikyon, hoping to distract her, he began to speak of their soon-arriving child, and the hopes and dreams they would have for him (or her).

Aelia's emotional pain subsided a bit, and though she tried not to give in to the temptation, she turned behind when Gaius wasn't looking to take one last glance at the poor baby girl she feared would die from exposure or by wild dogs. Her heart jumped, though, when she saw a man and woman by the crate, with two children of their own standing beside them, holding the baby in their arms. Maybe there was hope after all.

They looked like foreigners to her—so many traveled this area since the emperor cleaned out the southern Mediterranean of rebels, but she could see them smiling as they held the baby. For some unknown reason, she felt they were good people and the baby would be all right. Though the woman was holding the child, her husband was also focused on the infant, making faces, and bringing his own children in to see the baby.

Their behavior didn't suggest they were looking for a future slave; it seemed more altruistic than that. Before Aelia and Gaius turned the corner, the woman holding the baby girl looked up, met Aelia's gaze, and nodded. Aelia was a bit taken aback by the woman's response to her.

She wondered why they chose to take the baby girl in despite the cost and complications. She wondered why some people abandoned their children and why others took them into their households. She wondered why these people had kept the baby while they put her back down.

Aelia didn't know the answers, but deep inside, she felt a yearning to be someone who gave hope to the hopeless, and love to the unloved.

Not to any god in particular, she asked for assistance in becoming that person, no matter what the cost. Little did Aelia know that her prayer was heard, but that some good things are very costly indeed.

Chapter Four

Provocation

The red kitchen door swung open, and Matt marched into the room, dropped three empty cardboard boxes onto the checkered vinyl floor, and said, "Man, it smells like old person in here."

William was still sitting at the kitchen table, locked in fascination over their purported family story. He replied to Matt, "Good, good. More boxes," but never lifted his eyes from the letter.

"The question is, big brother. . ." Matt said, pulling a chair beside his brother, ". . . whether the smell is from this house, sweet old Uncle Lester, or you." William didn't bother to respond to his cheekiness. "What's that?" Matt asked, snatching the letter from William's grasp.

"That. . ." a frowning William said, carefully grabbing it back from Matt, ". . . is a very ancient letter that describes our family heritage. It is very fragile so treat it with care. It is more valuable than you know."

"Really!" Matt replied, his interest sparked. "How much is it worth?" He held out his hand and said, "May I please look at it, Professor Berrit?"

William smirked and handed the book over to his brother and said, "Depends upon whether or not it is an authentic letter of our family history going back to the time of Christ." Matt let out a whistle. "But you couldn't sell it and get enough money to buy yourself a Porsche. It has more nuanced, historical, and cultural value." Matt responded with a quiet raspberry.

Matt thumbed through a few of the pages, closed the book, set it down on the table, and slid it to his brother. "That. . . is incredibly dull, bro."

"It really isn't. From what I can tell so far, this book describes how our family first became Christians, and how that faith passed on from generation to generation."

"Until it got to me!" Matt proclaimed, with a slight bow of his head.

"That's not something to boast about," William replied.

"I'm pretty proud of it, bro, if you are fine believing those old fairy tales, whatever, but don't expect me to be such a sucker," Matt retorted. "I believe in real, empirical things that you can prove."

"Sure, Matt. Like life on other planets," William said, moving from the table to pick up two of the boxes.

"Hey, that's a mathematical certainty!" Matt replied, picking up the remaining box and following his brother into the hallway. "With so many galaxies, there has to be life like us out there. Carl Sagan said that the universe is bigger than anything the prophets delivered in the Bible and even more elegant."

"I don't necessarily disagree with that; there is just no hard, concrete evidence to back it up, and yet you still do. I can use the same line of reasoning to support belief in a divine being. Like John Lennox has said, you don't have to choose between God and the laws of physics, like they were in conflict. So, your dismissal of Christianity and my faith is illogical."

"Faith?" Matt said, chuckling. "You're not what I would call a die-hard believer, William."

William spun around and stood toe-to-toe with his brother. "At least, I occasionally go to church even after Mom and Pop died. When was the last time you heard a sermon or sung a hymn or. . ."

"Jesus, you are a hypocrite, " Matt blurted out. "You go on Christmas and Easter! And mainly because you feel guilty because of skipping out the rest of the year—admit it."

"One, don't take the Lord's name in vain; two, I go because I believe," William asserted.

Matt replied, "Uh-huh. Sure."

William tossed his boxes up into the attic, turned, and took the box from Matt's arms. "Ya know, Matt, sometimes you can be a shallow sacrilegious jerk." He saw a flash of anger in Matt's eyes and wondered if they would come to blows.

Matt took a deep breath, clapped the dust off his hands, and walked away, saying, "You know, William, sometimes you are an arrogant sanctimonious ass. I'm out of here."

"Oh, how sad," William replied, stomping up the attic stairs, box in hand. "But you know that I am right," he said, loud enough for Matt to hear it before the front door slammed.

He moved to where he found the letter in the old trunk and sat down on it. He ran his hand over his face and said to himself, "Quite mature, Dr. Berrit—you moron," feeling embarrassed at his response to his brother. He let his paternalism get the best of him again.

Deep down, he knew Matt meant well and was a good thinker, maybe even better than he in many areas, and yet William saw his brother struggling to find his vocation, never settling down in one place or with someone, and he worried about him. He thought about their exchange and considered how he could have handled it better. He also wondered how he could or should mend this little tiff—one of many in their past. But a more troubling realization occurred to him.

Matt had hit upon a significant truth about him. For a very long time, he had just been going to church out of obligation to the memory of his mother. Going to church had become more about social convention rather than pleasing his maker. The reality was that he found services boring and rote, and though in his youthful past he had found joy singing the hymns and choruses, they now just marked the minutes until the service was over and he could rush back home to watch the Ravens or Bo-Sox play during their perspective seasons.

William rubbed his beard, pondering his choices. Ironically, he felt he was at a religious crossroad. Maybe he would stop pretending to be a churchgoer, even during the holidays. Maybe it was time for him to show more integrity in his actions regarding God. He felt compelled to make a decision one way or another, but both choices felt wrong. He did believe in God, in a vague sense, but not personally, and definitely not with as much passion as the men and women he had read about in the letter.

He filled the box with old milk jugs of water dated September 1999 (sorry, Uncle Les, but you were wrong about Y2K and the end of the world) and carried it downstairs to the kitchen, which he knew was a silent excuse just to continue reading Great-Grandpa Alexander's letter.

Sitting at the kitchen table once more, he picked up the book and read on.

Chapter Five

The Cult

Walking home from the celebration, Alon saw the four Roman soldiers sitting in front of the fountain at the center square and tried to think of a route to get around them undetected. Every city had a garrison of these grizzled yet professional warriors sent to maintain the *Pax Romana*—the so-called "Peace of Rome"—which was more about oppression than harmony. These men were to be feared and obeyed but never loved; they were avoided like the death itself.

He wondered what they wanted from the citizens of Larissa, but decided he didn't want to know. Grabbing Naamah's hand, he maneuvered them behind some carts selling linens and fruit and tried to slip through the center unnoticed.

"Stop right there, citizen!" a voice bellowed from a portico to Alon's right. A Roman soldier emerged from the shadows, taking a last bite from a piece of pork before tossing it into the street. He wore a silver helmet with gold accents; it was clear he held higher authority than the other soldiers.

Alon tried to change his look of alarm to one of affinity. "How can I help you, sir?"

He walked up to them and stood within inches of Alon. To Naamah, he looked ten feet tall, and his armor gleamed in the afternoon sun. She noticed his short sword hanging by his side. It looked sharp and discolored but had some nicks in it up and down the blade. "Have you your *libellus*?" he asked Alon.

"I'm. . . I'm sorry, sir, but I don't know what that is," Alon replied in a shaky voice.

"Your libellus, *muris*—your certificate of worship for your fine and blessed imperator, Nero. We have just started this dictum in this province. All over the Mediterranean, the emperor is worshipped as a god. The god."

"I. . . am a Jew, sir. We are forbidden from such practices and have accommodation from Rome, I think."

"He's no Jew!" Alon heard a woman's voice shriek from behind him. An old woman working a nearby cart, covered in a black shawl, shuffled up to them and poked Alon in the chest. "He's a Christ-follower. Cursed."

The Roman soldier cocked his head and said, "You follow Christus Rex? Or are you a friend of Caesar?" Alon saw the soldier pat his sword handle and felt the sweat pour from his head, as a dark fear filled his core.

"No, sir. The old woman is incorrect. I am a Jew. I follow Yahweh. As so does my daughter here. *Ego sum amicus de Caesar.*"

The soldier looked at Alon, then squatted down to face level with Naamah and smiled. "Tell me, *puella*, do you believe in Iesous Christus?"

Naamah looked at the soldier and then to her father, who was ever-so-slightly shaking his head, and she said, "No. We don't follow. . . Iesous." Alon breathed a quiet sigh of relief until he heard his daughter say, "We follow Yeshua!"

The old woman threw up her hands and said, "You see? He's a blasphemer and an enemy of Rome." Then she spat at their feet. "Just like Eldad, that sorcerer. Traitors to us all!"

Alon didn't make a move. The soldier's smile disappeared, and he stood up. He spoke to Alon in an official, emotionless tone. "You both need to come with me." He took Alon by the arm and pulled him along. Naamah grabbed her father by the hand and said, "Where are we going, father?"

"Quiet child," Alon responded.

The soldier pushed Alon to a table in front of the fountain. Two of the soldiers were seated; the other two were standing on guard, spears and shields ready for action. There were wooden cages of birds behind them, and a flint knife and bronze platter rested on the green painted table. Alon saw bloodstains on the paver stones beneath their feet.

"This man. . . and his lovely daughter. . . want to offer sacrifice to the emperor. Give him a bird."

"Yes, Captain Primus."

Primus turned to Alon. "Do you have any money?"

Alon replied, "Not on me, sir."

Primus reached into a pocket and handed his lieutenant a coin. "Then permit me this first time."

The other seated soldier reached behind him and pulled a white dove from a cage. He held it out to Alon and said, "Do you want to kill it or shall we?"

Alon hesitated for a moment, but then he said, "You do it."

The soldier held the bird down on the platter, picked up the knife, and put it to the dove's neck. He looked at Alon and commanded, "Now swear allegiance to Caesar, your lord."

Alon said nothing, head down. Primus leaned close to Alon and whispered in his ear, "If you don't do this, then your daughter will see us kill you, and then she will be enslaved. Just say, 'Caesar is Lord,' and you can go."

Knowing he had little choice, Alon raised his head a bit and said with no conviction, "Caesar. . . is. . . Lord." The soldier sliced off the head of the dove with one quick slice. Immediately, Alon felt disgrace for denying the savior. Eldad and Barnabas would be ashamed to call him friend now. Yeshua's sacrifice had been in vain for him.

Primus slapped Alon on the back and said, "See, *muris*? So easy and you're on your way." He handed him a piece of paper with the word, *"Lebelli"* on the top, and then pushed Alon from the table, but gently patted Naamah on her bottom and said, "Farewell, daughter of Yeshua."

Naamah didn't know how to respond to the soldier man or what she had just seen, but she said, "Thank you, sir." Alon started walking through the city center toward home in shock and dismay, with his daughter trailing behind him. Alon's regret was interrupted, once again, by the shrieking of the old woman.

"Traitor! You call yourself a Jew, and then worship Caesar as a god! You are a blasphemer!" Alon tried to move past her, but she blocked his exit and grabbed on to his tunic. He swatted her hand away from his clothing, and she slapped him across the face. He became enraged and pushed her to the ground. Why in Hades did she care about what they believed anyway? She landed with a thump and then began to wail. "It's none of your business, *zkenah!*"

Soon, other men and women were yelling and striking at Alon. He looked for a quick route out, but all their exits were blocked. He kept envisioning poor Eldad being beaten to death by the mob, and he shuddered deep inside in fear for himself and for Naamah, who was being shoved around, too, by the angry crowd.

Someone tripped Alon and he fell down, pulling Naamah with him, the side of his head hitting the hard paver stones. He was stunned and he felt blood streaming down the side of his face. He was conscious, but everything become blurry and muffled. He felt the mob kicking and hitting him all over; their voices sounded ghostly and demonic. He was terrified, but deep inside, he knew he had to protect Naamah. He heard her whimpering, so he pulled her even closer and used his body to block blows meant for her.

Then the assault stopped, and he heard his attackers start to scream and cry in fear and pain. Glancing up, he saw the five Roman soldiers beating men and women alike. One of them kicked the old shrieking women in the stomach, and she fell down and didn't move at all. The soldiers used their shields to bludgeon people to the ground, and the handles of their swords to strike the agitators in the nose and mouth. It was a bloody effective way to disperse an angry unarmed crowd.

At first, Alon thought the Roman guard was there to rescue them, but he soon realized they were being arrested for disorder when the soldiers lifted both Alon and Naamah to their feet before putting the chains on their wrists. The soldiers then led them to a prison coach, where other people were also shackled and detained.

Through the caged walls of the coach, Alon saw the soldier who forced him to worship Nero walk by, and he cried out to him, "Captain Primus! Please! We are innocent. We were attacked for no good reason."

Primus stopped and looked at him with cold gray eyes. He replied, "Perhaps. But if one innocent lamb causes ten hungry wolves to begin fighting for its flesh, it is easier to remove the lamb than make the wolves not be wolves."

"But my daughter, please! She can't go to jail. She's only three years old."

At this, Primus walked to the cage and said, "If we let her go, she will tell others what has happened, and then we will have even more agitators to deal with. No, *Muris*. You brought her into the trap—not I." With that, he mounted his horse and galloped off before the jail carriage.

Naamah clung to him, weeping and crying out, "Oh, Daddy! Make them stop! Where's Momma?" She only stopped crying when she fell asleep out of emotional exhaustion. He thought, *Poor Naamah. What had she done to deserve this?*

Alon slumped down in the bench and pondered their predicament. He could understand if God was punishing him. After all, he had let his wife, Meira, die, and he had lied about following Yeshua when he knew he should be truthful, but Naamah was blameless. She deserved a better life than this. What was Yahweh doing? He felt confused, abandoned, and angry.

Despite his agitation, Alon prayed to Yahweh there in the caged coach. More than any plea he had ever done before, he came before the Lord, the true Lord, and begged for mercy and deliverance from this evil place—not for his sake, but for his sweet innocent Naamah.

Chapter Six

Desperation

Less than a mile from her parent's home, Aelia began bleeding from her womb. Gaius cursed at himself for letting her sway his decision to make such a long journey by foot, but they were both so joyous at the advent of this child. Aelia told him she was strong enough to make the half-day journey, and truth be told, her pregnancy glow seemed to back up her claims.

Now, however, Gaius could see that the heat and terrain were too much for his wife to endure in her delicate state. He helped her sit under a shady olive tree before running the mile to his father-in-law's villa to ask for help. With a disappointing grimace from his father-in-law, Justus, he and Gaius climbed into a horse-driven cart, rushing to rescue Aelia.

The ride back to the villa was not filled with much conversation (not that her father spoke much to her anyway), but they did discuss having the local physician come visit to examine her. Justus informed Gaius that the man was good but expensive, and that he didn't intend to pay for it. His daughter's malady was caused by Gaius's reckless disregard for her safety and his foolishness in not weighing the consequences of such a journey in her current state. Gaius didn't argue with him at all.

Once Aelia was resting in her old bedroom in the villa, with her mother nursing and consoling her, Gaius rode off to procure the services of the physician, Menander, and to purchase the needed medicinal herbs for his wife. True to Justus's words, the cost for the medical care of his wife was very expensive, and a brief pause at the Temple of Helios to offer a sacrifice to the gods so that they would look with favor upon their circumstance only added to the expenses.

The physician was from Ephesus, and he arrived at the villa that night with a female assistant—his wife, Phoebe. After examining Aelia and applying the first dose of his curative elixir, he spoke to Gaius and her parents in the courtyard.

"Thank you, dear physician, for coming out to take care of our beloved daughter," Justus gushed to Menander, tears in his eyes.

"No worries, my friend," Menander replied. "I am just amazed that the baby still lives within her. Most would have lost the child by now. Some would have perished from the ordeal."

Justus shot an angry glare towards Gaius, who deflected the silent criticism with praise of his own. "Yes, honorable doctor. We are so blessed to have you here to help my poor wife. My father, Justus, was right to have so much faith in you. Clearly, you have saved my wife and my child, and for that I will be forever grateful."

"Well," Menander responded, "let's wait and see what the night holds. I and my wife will stay by Aelia's side until we are sure she is stabilized, but she will need to continue to take the herbs I have prescribed to prevent the child from sloughing off in the womb."

Aelia's mother joined in and asked, "For how long, dear sir?"

"Unfortunately, we have found that pregnant women with this condition must take the elixir the entire pregnancy until the baby is delivered. Ceasing the prescription just brings on another bleeding episode, and one more severe."

"She will have the elixir; the cost is irrelevant," Gaius said, more for his father-in-law's benefit than for Menander's. "Nothing is more important to me than the life of my wife and my child."

The three men shared a glass of wine and toasted to the gods before Menander returned to Aelia's room to check up on her. Once he left, Gaius began discussing Aelia's convalescence with Justus. Both men looked and felt exhausted.

"Father, I know how much you care for Aelia, and for that I am grateful."

"Thank you, Gaius. I am sorry if I was too harsh to you before. I just hate to see my daughter suffer, but I understand the persuasive power of a beautiful wife."

"Beautiful and brilliant, sir, but I am determined that both Aelia and the child will live."

Justus shook Gaius's hand and said, "That cheers my heart more than you know, son. I never doubted your kindness and capability to care for my daughter. That still holds true today."

The two moved to the dining area and reclined on the floor cushions as they sipped their wine and nibbled on cheese and bread.

Gaius stared at the wall as he considered his next steps.

"The medicinal herbs Menander requires are very expensive—they are shipped from Carthage, which gets it from deep within the African demesnes. The chemist tells me that the plant only grows on the plains of a far-off desert, and the product is delivered quite sporadically; thus, the exorbitant cost."

Justus took a sip of wine and then asked, "Can you afford to buy the herb for the entire pregnancy? I am not sure we have much to spare with the damage to our vineyards from the drought."

"I can purchase enough for now, but I will need to go back to work to afford it for another seven months. I hope that you could look after Aelia when I go."

"What will you do, my son?" Justus asked.

Gaius picked up the cheese knife and replied, "What I do best, father. What I did best before I married your daughter."

"You will reenlist? That might carry you far away to the edges of the empire."

"No, Justus. I was thinking of something closer to home—the amphitheater in Pompeii."

"You would become an auctorati? A gladiator? That's a dangerous business, my boy."

"True, but I think it worth the risk, considering how much it pays off. I saw several gladiatorial fights while in the army. It doesn't take much to defeat the dregs being executed nowadays. And, I have friends— former soldiers in my company—who work at various gladiator schools as *lanistae* who would help with my training."

"I never knew you were this capable, Gaius," Justus said, smiling.

Gaius stabbed the cheese block and left the knife wobbling back and forth. "I do what needs to be done, Justus. I had hoped to never kill again, but Aelia needs me to do this to save her life and the child's. Besides, the gods will no doubt favor us even more for sending some wretched criminals to Hades, where they belong."

Justus finished his wine and rose, saying, "Come, let's go see how our treasured Aelia is doing."

"Good idea, father. One thing, though," Gaius asked before gulping down the rest of his wine. "Please don't let Aelia know what I will be doing. I think it would upset her too much, worrying about me all the time. Let's merely tell her that I am being engaged as a military consultant."

"A brilliant move, son," Justus affirmed. "Now you are thinking about the consequences before actions. You are a wise man indeed."

"Thank you, honorable Justus," Gaius replied, bowing to him. Justus bowed back and left the room.

As Gaius followed his father-in-law, he considered the irony of him taking lives in order to save lives. It was an enigma of virtuous violence. Plato would approve of his actions, especially because gladiatorial combat only rid the cities of destructive criminals, but he wondered what it would be like to kill for sport, even though the men (and women?) were criminals.

He tried not to think about it too much in the next weeks that followed. *"The conscience slows the sword,"* his former legion commander had said to him. Try as he might, though, the words of Cicero taught to him by his *doctore* decades earlier kept appearing in his thoughts. "The wise are instructed by reason, average minds by experience, the stupid by necessity, and the brute by instinct." He wondered which one he was now and which one he could become in the near future.

Chapter Seven

Unsettling

William finished reading the chapter in his great-great uncle's letter and closed the ancient book with delicate care. His eyes stung and he rubbed them, unsure of how long he had been reading these stories of his purported ancestors. He looked up at the wall clock and saw it was three in the morning. He had been reading solid since 10:00 p.m.

William was fascinated by the letter, and he felt compelled to keep exploring it. Even now he wanted to dig deeper into the next chapter— but he didn't know if his curiosity was more professional or personal. He was, after all, a history professor, and this book presented a cultural snapshot of Mediterranean life, of what an early believer could have experienced in the first century CE.

Life in the ancient Roman Empire could be as cutthroat and cold-blooded as this story suggested it to be. Still, years of academic training instilled in him a cynical and skeptical attitude toward works of antiquity. His PhD supervisor was an ardent deconstructionist who would have (no doubt) ripped the letter to shreds for its singularity of truth. But this writing did not seem to be a fanciful myth, created to sooth (or deceive) the hearts and minds of the reader. If anything, it agitated William to his core with its dark, painful presentation of reality. The characters were not heroes of old, which he would have preferred. He could easily imagine himself doing the same things if he was in the same circumstances, and that thought troubled him.

He wasn't sure if it was because of the recent deaths of his parents or Uncle Les, or because of his ongoing discussion/debates over God with his brother Matt, but this letter had triggered something deep in William, and he still didn't know if it was a good or bad thing. He had felt comfortable before in his perfunctory relationship with God, but this letter had begun to undercut his former posturing, making him uncomfortable in his faith and the listlessness of his "life." Matt was right—William was hardly what one would call a believer. He was more like an appeaser to God, the memory of his parents, and his guilt. This letter called him out on it.

Glancing at the clock again and remembering his early morning class at 10:00 a.m., he grabbed the letter, placed it in his briefcase, and went home to his studio apartment. On the drive home, he determined to do two things later in the day: one, he would send an e-mail to his brother saying he was sorry things got so heated, and, two, he would put off grading the midterm papers until he finished reading the damn letter. It was too distracting not to finish it; he wanted some closure in the matter.

Arriving home, he saw Claudius, his Australian shepherd, peering out of the skinny front doorway window—the dog's one red eye glowing from the light of his headlights (the dog's other eye was blue). Since William's recent breakup with Reneé, his girlfriend and fiancée of six years, Claudius had been William's buddy and confidant in his unexpected bachelorhood. Fortunately for William, Reneé never liked Claudius (a vestige of William's pre-engaged freedom), and let William keep the hairy protector of the Berrit household. Reneé took the calico cat, though, much to William's relief.

Claudius yelped with delight as his master came home, and William set down his briefcase before doing his compulsory one-minute wrestling match on the floor with the dog. Then he let the dog out, drank a huge class of milk, and headed up to bed. Throwing his clothes in the corner near the laundry hamper (Reneé had trained him well), he collapsed into his forever unmade bed, set the alarm on his iPhone, and fell asleep the moment his mousy brown head hit the pillow.

Even if he had hit the snooze on his iPhone four times, William did get into his office with a half hour to spare before class. So he sat down at his desk in his small windowless office in the old history building on campus and turned on his iMac. A loud ding indicated he had e-mail. He turned on the program and saw several desperate messages awaiting him from students explaining their absences, bad scores, or future paper plans, but he also noticed an e-mail from Matt.

Opening it, he got a lump in his throat as he read.

Dear Willbo—

Please forgive me for judging your faith or your walk with your God. I had no right to disrespect you, bro. That was wrong of me and I know you mean well (so do I!). We shouldn't let religion get in the way of our friendship and brotherhood.

I was wondering if you would like to come with me to the Westside Science and Religion Group tomorrow night—a freethinker by the name of Barker will be speaking and discussing his book, God is Not Great. I think you might enjoy the discussion.

Love you, dweeb.
(St.) Matthew

William clicked on "REPLY" and wrote,

Dear St. Matthew—

I would love to attend the pagan gathering with you tomorrow night. It has been some time since I have seen anyone sacrifice to the great non-God of science. I hope that I am not your main offering, of course.

I am sorry that I spoke down to you last night, pal. You are a smart guy and really irritating, sometimes, but I love you (dork). I appreciate the invite.

Dr. William F. Berrit,
PhD in History and Haughtiness

William hit "SEND," and noticing the time, he gathered his lecture notes, opened his briefcase, and tossed them inside. Seeing the letter, he pulled it out of the briefcase and put it into his top desk drawer. It was a bit silly, but he felt he needed to protect it from unauthorized eyes. Moreover, he felt he had first rights on this historical treasure because, one, he made the discovery, and, two, it concerned the faith of his family. He did resolve to show it to the chair of the department when he finished reading the letter to get her take on the book. Someone else needed to authenticate it in due course—but not yet.

With a "Yikes!" for his lateness, William rushed off to teach on Hellenistic Greece to forty-five teenage would-be scholars of indeterminate attentiveness.

Chapter Eight

The Jail

Alon sat on the wet dirt floor, his back leaning against the slimy cold rock walls of the jail. One long chain had been threaded through an iron hoop embedded in the wall four feet up from the ground, and manacles on each end of the chain secured his wrists in a sort of pouncing position. It wasn't much of a jail—it was more like a bricked-in cave—but it still felt like it was one wall removed from the gates of Hades. It was dark and smelled like blood, and it felt airless. Alon would have vomited if he had any food in his stomach, but they hadn't eaten for some time.

Naamah was unchained and was curled up in a ball in his lap. The Roman guards were unconcerned about her escaping, and Alon had no idea where they were at any more. Their journey in the caged coach lasted over a day, and he had passed out for a while due to the heavy heat of the countryside. He only awoke when they pulled the prisoners out of the coach to relieve themselves and to drink from a dirty water bucket. Still not aware of their dire situation, Alon worried about his daughter getting ill from the brackish water.

He could hear Naamah whimpering in her sleep, and he managed to move one hand down to stroke her head in comfort by raising his other arm high above, which allowed the chain to slide down. He was unable to figure out any way to rescue them from their predicament. He had heard no talk of prefects or judges from his captors, and any requests for information had been met with a sharp poke from the end of a spear. Alon hadn't felt this sad and hopeless since the night his beloved Rachel had died from the plague.

Despite the darkness, he could see some of the faces of other prisoners. Most looked as horrified as he imagined he did—torn from their homes and normal lives, thrust into this nightmare—but one in particular looked angry and menacing. Alon felt the hair on the back of his neck stand straight up, as if he were suddenly face-to-face with a ravenous lion. The angry man's eyes grew wild when he noticed Alon' gaze, and he growled, "Keep looking at me, Christus, and I'll be the last person that you ever see." The man turned his gaze to Naamah, "and then I'll take a bite of your daughter for dessert."

Alon lifted his hand from Naamah's head, made it into a defiant fist, and replied with calm, yet threatening finality. "Touch her and I will kill you."

The man lifted his head up and snorted in laughter. "You will have to outrace the Romans for that right, Christus." Alon hoped the nasty man would be dispatched soon.

Their threatening exchange was interrupted by the clanging of keys and the screeching of the rusted metal jail door as it swung open. A Roman guard came in with a bucket of water and a bag of bread for the six captives inside. He first walked to Alon and Naamah, and he gave them each a cup of the water, which tasted so cool and sweet, compared to the earlier drink that Alon nearly cried. The guard then handed them two pieces of bread, which the two wolfed down in abandon. Alon mustered enough courage to ask, "Please, sir, can my daughter have another cup of water? It is so hot in here. I am worried about her."

The guard frowned, but relented and gave Naamah another cup, to which she replied, "Oh, thank you, sir." Alon's eyes welled with tears and nodded to the guard who nodded back.

The angry prisoner yelled, "Hey, Roman ass! Give me my share, too, or do you just like young flesh?"

The guard walked over to him and kicked him in the leg, yelling back, "Shut up, Ze'ev, or you won't get anything at all."

As the guard turned his back to feed another prisoner, the angry man managed somehow to grab the ankle of the guard and trip him. Once down, the man pulled the guard's foot close enough to his face to bite down hard into his calf. The guard howled in pain, and two other guards rushed in to his aid.

The screaming of the guard set Naamah sobbing in terror. Alon turned his daughter's face away from the scene, which became brutal. The angry man's jaw was clamped down tight, and he wouldn't let go of the guard despite the kicks from both sides of him. Eventually, one of the guards used the butt end of his sword to strike the man in the mouth, and red teeth flew everywhere, releasing the cursing and writhing injured guard. The two soldiers dragged their wounded comrade out of the jail cell before coming back to punish the once angry man, Ze'ev, now whimpering and sobbing even more than Naamah.

When the chastising was over, the two soldiers left chuckling, and none of the other prisoners dare lift their eyes, lest they invite a battering of their own. Naamah's head was buried into her father's shoulder, and she kept repeating, "Home, Daddy. Home, please. Home. . ."

All Alon could say was, "Soon, Ahuvi, soon," and then he cried with her, trying to hug her despite his shackles.

When she had fallen asleep from exhaustion, Alon laid her down in his lap again and glanced over to Ze'ev. Alon noticed the prisoner next to the beaten man leaning over him. First, he thought the other prisoner was going to finish the job the soldiers had started, but he soon realized the man was just tending to Ze'ev's wounds. After lifting Ze'ev to the cot he had been sitting on, the man lifted a cup of the remaining water in the bucket to Ze'ev's lips.

"Not too much," he said to Ze'ev.

Ze'ev found it hard to speak but muttered, "Why. . . helping. . . me?"

The other prisoner began to wipe the blood from Ze'ev's face and replied, "Have mercy on some who doubt; save others, snatching them out of the fire; and on some, have mercy mixed with fear, hating even the garment polluted by the flesh."

Through his wheezing, Ze'ev asked, "Who. . . are. . . you?"

The other prisoner replied, "The name's Silvanus, friend. I'd like to talk to you about God."

Ze'ev first grimaced, gurgled, and spat out blood, and then said with a weak chuckle, "There is no escape, Silvanus. Don't you know that?"

Looking deep into Ze'ev's fearful eyes, Silvanus smiled at the man and said to him, "Let me tell you a story, brother, of a man from Israel who will make you believe in perfect deliverance once again. You won't have to fear death anymore."

Ze'ev did not waste any more words; he knew the fates, Atropos in particular, had decided to cut off his life string this time, no doubt because of his foolish, murderous choices that had landed him in this jail. His past responses to religious zealots was to strike them down and strip them of all they possessed—rather ironic, considering that this believer had lifted him up and was freely sharing his coveted jail bed and precious water with him. Perhaps it was his fear or certainty that he was about to close his eyes for the last time, but he felt an overwhelming urge to listen to the man. And he did.

In fact, all the prisoners listened to Silvanus tell Ze'ev about hope in the desperate, murky shadows, and, for a brief moment, before Ze'ev drew his last breath and Silvanus wiped his bloody face with his tears, Alon remembered the joy of his beating heart when he first heard Eldad tell him long ago about the obscure Jewish carpenter who died so that no one would truly die again—if they just believe.

There, chained to the wall, with his poor helpless daughter clinging to him for safety and protection in this wretched cell with wretched violent men, it seemed that Alon was faced with two options only—both difficult to embrace. He could believe in God, believe in Yeshua as his deliverer who had brought him and his innocent daughter to this hellhole, or he could believe that the darkness had won again, as it had with martyred Eldad and his plague-stricken wife, and that there was no God or gods intervening in the lives of petty mortals. Life was brief joy surrounded by enduring pain and suffering.

Hope or misery, joy or sadness—the reality of his earthly world crashed down around him, suffocating him. He and Naamah were going to die. He wanted to pray to God, to praise him for His goodness and then to beg for mercy, but all he could say was, "Yeshua. Yeshua. Why?" He closed his eyes and felt the tears pour down his face, salty and bitter, moving as his soul toward final resignation and despair. He had gone as far as he could go on his own.

Chapter Nine

The Spectacula

Gaius entered into the *Pompeii Spectacula* for the first time in ten years. He and his fellow *auctoratae* strode in with confidence and pride, the sunlight shimmering off their silver and gold armament. Each one had his weapon drawn high above their heads, swinging them back and forth to the shouts and screams of the amphitheater's raucous crowd of 20,000 men and women ready for the excitement of the entertainment.

Gaius had to admit to himself that he always liked this part of the circus—it made him feel like the son of *Mars*. In the arena, he was the mighty warrior defeating all the enemies of Rome—both beast and barbarian. He had dispatched his share of lion and criminal in his gladiatorial career, but he had done it before as a youth, filled with wind, wine, and wishes of glory. Now, he just wanted to keep his child and his wife alive.

Once the preliminary parade ended, he and two other of his comrades stood *in statione,* sword and shield in hands, as the sounds of roaring beasts echoed out of the small tunnel at the northern end of the amphitheater. They could hear the animals charging toward them, mad with anger and hunger, which always made them braver in battle with the gladiators.

Gaius saw the great male lion emerge first, his orange mane about his face like the crown of Apollo himself. He was followed behind by a leopard and the ugliest hyena he had ever seen. Gaius moved in the path of the colossal feline beast—this was a noble creature to vanquish for the crowd—let the other *auctoratae* take the other animals; this was his kill.

Gaius and the lion squared off, each circling the other, looking for weaknesses before pouncing. The lion gave a loud roar that elicited an even louder roar from the crowd. Gaius looked into the lion's golden eyes and bellowed, *"Ego vincere, Leo!"* and then charged the cat. The crowd went wild with excitement.

Gaius had been trained by the best, and he knew how to kill the animal instantly, but that wasn't the point of the *Spectacula*. He needed to extend the battle, extend the wounding and the struggling for life, mimicking personal danger and peril, so that the final blow into the heart of the lion would evoke an explosion of euphoria from the mob. They wanted him to be a hero, and he gave it to them in expert fashion. No one ever criticized his performance in the arena.

When he charged the lion, it reciprocated, and the two came together with a loud crash of fur, fury, and blood as Gaius's sword sliced into the sinews of the cat's muscled shoulder before he slipped out of reach of those ferocious claws. The lion's roar changed from pride to rage, and Gaius knew he had brought out the ferocity of this king of the savannahs. The two exchanged blows for several minutes, until Gaius felt the crowd was ready. He lowered his guard for a moment and saw that the lion would take the bait.

With natural lethality, the lion leaped high into the air over Gaius, claws extended, giant mouth open, razor-sharp teeth itching to sink into the gladiator's soft unprotected neck. Gaius, though, was no wildebeest; he was a Roman conqueror—the undefeatable soldier. He dropped to his knee, raised his shield over his head, and then, at the last moment, he thrust his sword upward into the massive chest of the beast, which landed on top of him. A great cloud of dust hid the conclusion of this conflict of warriors.

The crowd stayed hushed as they waited for the dust to clear. The lion lay still, motionless in the amphitheater floor. When the silence inflated the curiosity of the multitude standing on their toes to see the carnage, Gaius rolled out from under the great slaughtered beast with a roar of his own, covered in blood. And the arena went wild. Once again, Gaius had won over the crowd; he knew his purse would be large tonight. The legate of Pompeii loved a happy, drunk, celebratory crowd, and he rewarded well those who added to the success of the local economy. Gaius chopped off one of the ears of the lion and flung it up into the front seats, to the delight of the young flirtatious girls screaming to him and baring their breasts, before following the other *auctoratae* back into the barracks to retire for the night.

His work in the arena was over for the moment—it was time to rest and recover at home for the next month's demonstration. Handing Gaius his share of the profits for the week's performance, his *lanista* informed him that in the next gladiatorial pageant in Thessalonica, he would be the chief executor of a band of Jewish rebels creating chaos in the empire with their worship of an inconsequential rebel from Jerusalem.

Gaius had no problem killing the enemies of Rome, although he had never executed anyone for religious reasons. Regardless, he submitted to the authorities above him, which was reasonable and beneficial to a smooth-running society. If that meant killing men, women, and even children for the good of Rome, he would comply. It wasn't pleasant, but it was necessary.

On the way to the baths to clean up, Gaius walked past the convicted and caged men, women, and children who would soon be stalked and murdered by other wild animals—wolves, bulls, and even a wild boar—and other gladiators for the amusement of the mob. He thought nothing of them; he heard neither their cries for help nor their appeals to God, but he did feel a sense of urgency to get to the *pharmacopola* to get his wife's medicine.

He prayed that the gods would let their baby live and that he (or Aelia) hadn't angered them in some unknown way. Much like dealing with the principate or local governors, the gods were fickle and punished with discrimination if not adequately appeased. He committed to behaving at his best for the next five months to placate them. Perhaps then, a child of theirs would survive, but, in honesty, he felt little hope for the future. He would try, though. That was the best he could do for his wife and their unborn child.

Chapter Ten

The Other Physician

Aelia's bleeding and cramping had begun to increase in the last week or so. Even though the physician, Menander, seemed confident that day when he came to visit and spoke some comforting words to her, she saw the worry in his eyes and suspected things were going badly when he upped the dosage and confined her to bed until she was stabilized.

Adding to her anxiety, his bedside manner was less than inspiring. She wondered how someone purported to be so smart could talk so little. She tried several times to strike up a conversation with him, but he just ignored or dismissed her views, preferring to talk with her stern father, Justus, instead.

"Try not to fret too much over the baby, Aelia," Menander said to her. "Matters such as these are too complex for the feminine psyche, dear child. Just trust in the gods, your father, and me, and all will be well."

"But. . ." she began.

Aelia's father wagged his finger at her and said, "You hear that, daughter? No worrying—physic's orders."

"Abba. . ." she began, but he gave her his pater-potentate look, and she knew to say no more. Instead, she gave him an insolent smile and wanted to hurl some insults (and a chair) at them for their condescension. Her father had always patronized her growing up, and it angered her that he considered women to be so inferior. Gaius just blamed it on his generation and the culture. Aelia could understand that, but it didn't make it any easier to endure.

Menander turned his attention to Aelia's father and said, "Justus, it is time for me to return to Ephesus. My wife and I want to get back before the rains begin."

Justus frowned but replied, "I know, my friend. You have been good to stay in town so long to care for my daughter. I just worry what will happen when you leave."

Menander opened his medical satchel and pulled out two small pieces of parchment. He handed the first one to Justus. "Here is my bill. You can pay me in installments, per usual, Justus. I know that you are good for it."

Justus nodded and took the parchment without looking at it. "Your skills deserve more coin than I can afford to give you, Menander, but I appreciate your generosity and flexibility."

Menander waved off Justus's compliments and said, "Pfft. Pfft. I am just a man with some life-saving knowledge of the body. And I am sorry that I must leave your family; however, I do have some good news."

"Yes?" Justus asked.

Menander handed him the other piece of parchment and said, "I have contacted a friend of mine from Macedonia—another fine physic—who is very willing to come check on Aelia next Sunday. He will make sure that the dosage is still working and the baby is doing well. Lately, he has been living in Philippi, so it is not too much of a journey for him. Plus, his costs are much more affordable than mine can be, especially considering your status and present station."

Aelia tried not to smile as she could tell her father was experiencing a taste of his own condescending medicine from the haughty physic. Justus managed a watered-down sarcasm. "Well, that's fortunate for the likes of us, then, mighty *Asclepius*."

Menander shook Justus's hand and said, "Good, good. I am off." Turning to Aelia, he told her, "Stay in bed. Obey your father, and the gods will see you through."

Aelia looked at her dad and saw him nodding, imploring her to acquiesce, which she obliged. She responded with a docile, "I submit to your authority, sir."

"That's a good girl, " he replied, patting her on the head as he left the room.

The next week went by without much improvement. In fact, though the bleeding abated a bit, Aelia's abdominal pain increased twofold. This proved problematic because Menander had also instructed her parents not to utilize the normal herbs for pain management, lest they cause more bleeding (or worse).

With Gaius gone, Aelia felt alone and miserable. Each night, her mother would come in to her room to assist her, but in truth, her mother had little emotional support to give to her daughter when the painful spasms returned. Her mother would say, "Oh, dear! I will go get you something for your forehead," and leave, only to have the servants return alone with the cold cloths. Aelia had learned long ago that her mother had a fragile sense of decorum, which real life shattered too easily.

Saturday night was the worst night ever for Aelia. The pain never ceased, and she cried for hours, trying to find a comfortable position, fearful of moving too much and hurting her unborn baby. It was a great relief then that the new physic arrived early in the morning to check on her. Justus wasted little time with introductions and libations, directing the physic to his daughter's room instead.

He was a tall man, slightly graying at the temples and was clean-shaven, except for a neat, well-groomed mustache. Despite her exhaustion, Aelia noted that the man's tan cloak had multiple repairs to it, but he still looked respectable.

The physic pulled a stool next to Aelia's bed and laid his medical bag on the table beside it. Without saying a word, he picked up a rag, dipped it into the basin of water by the bed, and wiped off her face and neck, as well as her arms. He pulled the bed cover down, and then washed her legs to her feet beneath her short nightgown. The cooling sensation brought immediate relief to Aelia, and she relaxed for the first time all night.

The physic put the wet cloth back into the basin and turned to her and said, "So, are you the young maiden who is with child?"

His unexpected candor made Aelia laugh, but she could tell that her father was irritated. This made her like the physic even more. She replied, "No, sir. I just ate some fruit with seeds, and apparently it sprouted inside my stomach."

"Well, it could have been worse. You might have swallowed an olive pit." The physic took her hand and said, "Hello, Aelia. My name is Luke."

Aelia started to reply, but a wave of pain interrupted the pleasantries.

Luke turned to Justus and said, "Bring me her medicine. And she needs some warm chicken broth. And a small glass of wine. Now."

Justus rushed off to gather his list, and Luke turned to Aelia, who was grimacing, clutching the bed rails, her knuckles turning white.

"I know it hurts, Aelia," Luke said. "But we will give you something to ease the pain." He began to examine her abdomen and delicate regions, but she was too distraught to feel any embarrassment.

Tears welled up in her eyes, and she grabbed Luke's arm. "I just don't want to lose the baby."

Luke took her hand in his and said, "Now, don't fret, dear woman," Luke said. "You will soon have a strapping son who will be wrecking your house. . . and all the hearts of the village girls."

Aelia smiled again, but another wave of agony hit her, and she tried her best not to curl up, whimpering. Luke spoke softly to her, "Aelia, can I try something with you? I would like to talk to God for you now, if you want."

Eyes closed, sweat beading on her forehead, and not really listening, Aelia said, "Whatever. . . helps. . ."

Luke placed his hands on her belly, closed his eyes, too, and was quiet for a minute before he started speaking.

"Dear God, our Father," he began. "We pray for this woman and the unborn baby inside her. We know that you came to earth long ago and endured the pain and suffering of being born a child for our sakes, to feel what we feel and be where we all were at one time in our lives. We pray that you take away Aelia's pain; that you heal her womb; that you rescue her baby from *abortio*. You are the God of life, not death. You came to heal all wounds. We know that you can do all things, *Christos*, because you conquered all wounds, even unto death. So, be with us tonight. Help me abound more in knowledge and depth of insight, and help this woman focus on what is joyfully ahead of her, not behind. Help her press on to the end to meet your gift to her—her child—who begun in love and restoration long ago. Thank you for hearing our prayers. Thank you for caring for us. In Yeshua's name, Amen."

When Luke finished the prayer, he found Aelia staring at him with wide eyes.

"How do you feel, woman?" Luke asked.

"What. . . happened. . . to me?" she asked in astonishment.

"I just prayed for you, sister—to my God, to the one God."

She looked at him, her face beaming. "The pain is gone, and I just felt the baby move."

Luke bowed his head, gave a victorious fist pump to the sky, and said, "Yes, Lord!"

Still in amazement and feeling better than she had felt well ever, Aelia said, "I don't understand." Luke smiled at her, and, as he reexamined her and found her bleeding had ceased, he told her of his travels to Antioch, where he met with a Jew named Paul who introduced him to the one true God of the heavens and the earth.

Aelia had extensive knowledge of all the Greek and Roman gods and goddesses, but she had never before heard of this deity. Being an intelligent woman, she knew the realities of the "powers" of the gods. She and her family had sacrificed thousands of pigeons to Zeus, Apollo, Demeter, Diana, Hermes, Poseidon, and the like, but with little to offer in the way of evidence for answered prayers. Furthermore, with the surreptitious assistance of a literate slave, she had learned to read and devoured whatever scrolls her father brought home from the *bibliotheca*. Thus, she had become an ardent cynic and skeptic, but this was something she could not argue against. This God had healed her.

By the time her father returned with the medicine, soup, and wine (which Luke consumed besides the medicine), Aelia had prayed with Luke and invited a new God—Yeshua—into her heart. Once again, her father looked annoyed as she told him what had just happened, and Aelia couldn't help but jump up and hug him and Luke. She and her baby had been healed.

After some cursory instructions from Luke to still take it easy for the baby's sake (and her parents), Aelia went back to bed. When Justus left the room to get Aelia's mother and to get Luke's fee, the physic pulled a scroll out of his medical bag and handed it to her.

"Here," he said. "This is a copy of a letter my friend Paul wrote to my *ecclesia*, my church. I think you will find it interesting. We can talk more about it when I return in a week to check your progress. Now, Aelia, you need to sleep. Please. Now."

Luke put the scroll under her pillow, pulled the covers over her, and said, "Good-bye, daughter of God."

Aelia closed her eyes and replied, "Good-bye, physic of God," and dozed off. With that, Luke gathered his things and left the room.

After a brief uncomfortable conversation with her parents who still were unsure of what had happened to their daughter, Luke mounted his horse and left the villa. Just outside, he passed by Gaius in his horse-drawn cart, returning home from his profitable business in the arena. Luke greeted him, introduced himself, and relayed the good healthy status of his wife and child. Gaius was pleased but suspicious of Luke's news. It sounded too good to be true.

Having a full education of Greek and Roman cultures, Luke saw the weapons in the back of the cart and inquired, "So, you are not a soldier. You must be an *auctorati*."

"Yes, your are astute, sir. I serve in the arena," Gaius responded with pride.

Luke shook his head and said, "How sad to make your living by killing people for sport."

Gaius bristled a bit and replied, "They all have it coming, physic. Besides, I dispatch whomever the emperor instructs me to. It is a legal affair."

Luke looked up at the sun and said, "I supposed God is served whether by life or by death." Then he turned his gaze to Gaius. "Still, I hope you find a way to escape your present situation. I sense you are a noble man, but the blood of the circus just cultivates selfish ambition, conceit, and the wrath of God, I believe."

"I do what I must," Gaius concluded.

"I can see that, friend," Luke stated. Raising his hand in farewell, Luke prayed, "Peace be to the brothers and love with faith," and then urged his horse forward.

Gaius returned with, "May Zeus guard your steps," as he snapped his horse with his whip.

Inside, Justus confirmed Luke's prognosis of his wife and child, and though Gaius was happy that her bleeding and pain were gone, he didn't like this new physic. He had heard Luke's blessing before in the arena, and he knew what sect it involved. He also didn't care for his opinion of righteous gladiatorial combat.

Luke was a Christian, which was a dangerous cult to be involved with, according to Rome. He himself had heard the rumors that they worshipped a dead crucified man, and ate his flesh and drank his blood. They were barbarians and needed to be exterminated if and when they got out of control. That was the role of the arena and the *auctorati*.

Luke, the physician, would be allowed to help his wife, but Gaius would watch him closely and provide a remedy of his own if matters became too menacing. Gaius had made a mess of things concerning Aelia before, and it nearly cost him her life and that of their child. He wasn't going to allow this man and his pernicious superstition to ruin the purity of his family life.

Chapter Eleven

Progress

William found it interesting that the local United Methodist Church had allowed the *Westside Science and Religion Group* to meet in their sanctuary, let alone the church building, considering the potential heretical discussions that were about to take place. This church in particular was started a century earlier by a Methodist Episcopal Church missionary, but it had undergone a revolution of sorts when a discontented Methodist minister by the name of Benjamin T. Roberts swept through the area in 1859, sharing his purist views of freedom for the believer.

In Roberts's view, the denomination had become corrupt with false teachings and unproductive emphases, and he and his followers promoted a better path to righteousness and reality than the institutional church provided. They were formally chastised, shunned, and expelled from the annual conference, which gave fuel to their holy fire and cause. Not surprisingly, Roberts and his supporters formed a new branch of Methodism that focused on social freedoms along with spiritual enlightenment and sanctification. True spirituality should bring freedoms—not just obligations.

Ten minutes before the meeting, Matthew had met William outside the church, and the two gave each other their normal uncomfortable hug, lasting about two seconds that included three pats on the back apiece. The two had never been gushy about their affection for each other, although the love was there and deep.

Matthew pretended to punch his brother on the chin, and, in a Godfather-Mafia-style voice, said, "I'm so glad that you can do me this favor, Gumba."

William replied in kind. "If I do this favor for you, my brother, then someday I may call upon you to assist me, too. That day might not be today—"

"Yeah, yeah," Matthew interrupted. "Let's go inside before the good seats are taken."

The building itself was monumental, constructed when churches were meant to inspire and quiet by the tallness of their spires and the cost of their masonry. If not a church, William thought this building would have made a fine castle. The first pioneer parishioners must have been awestruck as the ten-foot tall front doors opened for the first time. They walked into the largest house of God they had ever seen to sit on cushioned pews and sing hymns accompanied by a pipe organ bigger than their entire house before a black-robed minister spoke to them of God's greatness and the greatness of need for Him.

Taking a seat near the back of the sanctuary (to the annoyance of his brother) and reading the flyer handed to him entitled, "Life Without God," William presumed this evening would not carry the same conviction of God. Over a hundred people were in attendance that night, and he was surprised when the church's minister introduced the speaker.

"Ladies and gentlemen," the minister said, smiling, "I'd like to thank you for coming tonight to hear our esteemed guest discuss his views on God and religion—something I have some interest in." The audience laughed at his understatement. "We live in a changing world, not just biologically or environmentally but also culturally and religiously, and Christopher Barker presents a powerful argument for the advancement of human thought and spirituality. Fifty years ago, our membership included 2,000 members; today, 350 parishioners showing up is a good Sunday. Our understanding of God has been evolving for 6,000 years, and we have come to a pivotal juncture in our lives that many want to hide from. But I think we'd be better as a faith-group to listen and learn from what others outside the church have to say about that which we take for granted or assume without much factuality, it seems. Of course, you didn't come to hear the minister speak." Polite laughter came from the audience again. "So, without further introduction, allow me to present Mr. Christopher Barker."

Barker walked up, and the audience gave him a standing ovation. Some even hooted for him. He and the minister shook hands. Barker gave him a brief but forced smile, and then proceeded to the pulpit, with notes in hand.

The middle-aged man with graying hair waved to the audience and said into the microphone, "You might not be so enthusiastic after the offering," inducing more applause and laughter echoing through the sanctuary. He motioned for them to sit down, which they did. William noted how happy most of the audience seemed, except for what looked like an old farmer sitting alone in the third row far to the right side of the room. His expression was more apprehensive and sorrowful.

Barker began, "Well, let's get started, shall we?"

He took a drink from a glass of water left for him on the pulpit and then stated, "In my latest book, *The Unimpressive God*, I have written: 'All religion was created in the past utilizing the insecurities and ignorance of the human species to help explain life and to comfort weak-minded people when emotional experiences overpower epistemological understanding. The most ignorant of elementary school children know more about the workings of our world and the universe than the infantile founders of the great faiths. Marx called religion the opiate of the masses. I consider religion more to be the embalming fluid of the unenlightened."

William shifted a bit in his seat with the caustic critique of the faith. Looking over, he saw his brother staring at Barker, captivated by his message.

Barker continued, "There are many reasons why human beings have celebrated a deity throughout the eons, but I reject the notion of a supreme powerful figure for a variety of reasons, most of which are backed up by science and empirical evidence. Christianity, Hinduism, Islam—all religions—have their foundations in the fanciful imaginations of their holy tome writers. And since time immemorial, these writers have promoted intellectual cowardice, exclusivism, callousness, and bigotry that their gods spoke mainly to them and solely gave them the way to eternal life. I consider this the ultimate in arrogance: that in our amazing universe filled with billions and billions of stars and planets, God cares only about this planet, and only gave his message of truth to—as I put it in my book—'semi-barbaric provincials in the desert wildernesses.'" The audience applauded once again.

Taking another drink of water, he continued, "Evolution—science—has demonstrated, conclusively, the mechanisms of life and biology that have brought us here to this present state of modernity and comforts. God did not create the telephone—we did. God did not invent the vaccine for polio—we did. God did not transport us to the moon and beyond—we made it there ourselves. The ancients needed god to survive but we do not. We have our intellect and our technological and moral progress to help us live our lives as we choose to, not according to the whims of some 'unsophisticated, uncivilized, volitionally subhumans' and their mythical god. As I said in my latest book, 'Religion has never produced true, beneficial morality or ethics; rather human morality is the foundation of all religions."

William looked over at the elder man near the front; he was sitting at the edge of the pew, his eyes also glued to the speaker.

"So, tonight, dear *Westside Science and Religion Group,* I appreciate your willingness to discuss and debate the realities of life and to resist the superstitious tales of the Bible and Christian leaders for over two thousand years."

"How do you know that the tales are not true?" the elderly man interjected.

Barker shielded his eyes and looked out into the audience. "What was that?"

The man in the audience stood up and spoke louder, "I said, how do you know that the biblical accounts are false?"

Barker gave a condescending smirk into his notes and replied, "Because I don't believe in fairy tales, sir. I believe in empirical facts and evidence."

"But were you there when Jesus performed his miracles?" the man asked.

"Of course not—neither were you," Barker chided.

The man nodded and said, "True, but how do you know for a fact that Jesus wasn't the Son of God?"

"Because there are no gods at all, sir," Barker responded. "Ergo, Jesus could not be the Son of God."

A few people clapped for his response. The man just shook his head and said, "But that isn't good scientific methodology, Mr. Barker. You have started with a conclusion and deny all evidence to the contrary."

"That's not true," Barker contended.

William could sense that Barker was getting irritated and wanted to move on with his presentation. The minister stood up, walked to the pulpit, and spoke into the microphone, "Mr. Barker, this is Dr.

Ernest King. He taught biology and chemistry at our high school and community college for thirty years and is a member of our church."

"Oh," Barker responded. "I had no idea this was going to be an official debate tonight with a prestigious member of the academy. Perhaps you would like to come up here and continue our dialogue."

William saw the old professor smile at Barker. He replied, "That won't be necessary, Mr. Barker. I am glad that you have come to share with us. It is just that your conclusions are so absolute, so final, and being a researcher and having done scientific experimentation for most of my vocational life, I find your approach to the notion of a supernatural being a bit. . . closed off."

"Closed off?" Barker challenged.

"Yes, sir. Would you consider the eyewitness testimony of the Christian writers authoritative or supportive to the idea that a deity exists?"

"Not at all," Barker responded. "They were never written by eyewitnesses. The early church added that material in post-Jesus crucifixion. They needed their own Caesar and gave the role to Jesus."

"Again, Mr. Barker, how do you know that they didn't witness the miracles of Jesus Christ and his followers? Why does it have to be a creation of the church?"

"That is a good question, Dr. King, but I can only believe that which I can measure and quantify. There is no way to absolutely confirm the amazing stories. As I said in my book, science is not a belief system like Christianity or Islam. Our principles are based on scientific, rational facts, and good mature thinkers resist anything that challenges the rationality of science, such as the Christian story. We do encourage free-thinking and open-mindedness and asking good questions, but your questions are tired and worn out. You have added nothing new to the argument."

"That might be true, Mr. Barker," Dr. King conceded. "I am no theologian or apologist. I am just testing your worldview parameters. But what would it take for you to believe the stories?"

Barker chuckled and said, "Ironically, Dr. King, it would take a miracle." The audience joined with him in laughter. "What you are asking me to do is to take the word of some church leaders who, two thousand years ago, claimed that a man did something that no one could do since or can do today. That makes no sense to me."

"I agree that your conclusions would be true, if Jesus was merely human, but what if he were also the Son of God? What if the Gospel of John's claims about Jesus' activities were true?" Dr. King asked.

"But I do not believe that they are true because they violate natural law," Barker replied.

"And all humans have to follow natural law, correct?" Dr. King clarified.

"Correct," Barker agreed.

With all the audiences' eyes on him, the professor stroked his beard for a moment and asked, "Do you believe there is life on other planets, Mr. Barker?"

Barker's eyes lit up, and he stated, "Yes, I do!"

"Could this life on other planets be further evolved than humanity is currently?"

Barker nodded in agreement. "That is a definite possibility."

"Might they have other ways of communicating and functioning that we earthlings do not?" Dr. King added.

"Yes, if their anatomy and mental faculties allowed it," Barker clarified.

"We are aware of three special dimensions—could there be more?"

"Absolutely," Barker responded, "but we cannot understand them yet."

"Then, if on earth, might an advanced being from another planet or dimension do things otherwise impossible for human beings?" Dr. King asked.

Barker paused, looked at the professor, and then asked him, "Are you saying that Jesus was E.T.?" The audience roared in laughter.

The professor smiled and said, "Nope. Jesus was a human being. . . and God, but if he was a multidimensional advanced being, he might have been able to do all the astonishing things you claim he could not—he did not do—on earth and still not violate the laws of universal physics."

Barker acquiesced but added, "Not if he was just a human being like the rest of us, Dr. King, and that is assuming that Jesus even existed."

"That is the question, isn't it, Mr. Barker?" Before Mr. King sat down, he said, "Thank you for taking my questions, sir. I appreciated your candor."

Barker gave a nod to the professor and replied, "I appreciated your attempt at critiquing widely accepted scientific methodology as well." Barker grabbed his notes and said, "Now, where were we?" And he launched off onto another deconstructionist/nihilistic attack on mainstream religion. For the rest of the presentation, King remained quiet but took a copious amount of notes.

When the presentation ended, William and Matthew lined up with the rest of the audience members to buy Barker's book and get his autograph. In the parking lot, Matthew said to William, "Wasn't he awesome? Isn't that the most intelligent discourse on the impotence of religion you have ever heard? Man! I totally connect with Barker."

William replied, "Yes. Barker was quite a dazzling speaker, but what did you think about the questions of the old professor?"

Matthew shook his head and said, "Like Barker said, the geezer added nothing new to the dialogue."

"I don't know, Matt. He brought up some pretty glaring problems with Barker's argument. There is a definite circular-reasoning aspect to discount all biblical stories about God and Jesus because you assume and begin with the assertion that no god exists."

"Nah. Barker is right. Empirically, you cannot prove Christianity or God is true."

"Maybe," was all William said in return. He decided not to pursue the line of discussion further. He appreciated he had to just let go of some things with his brother for the sake of peace.

William punched Matthew in the arm before getting into his car. "Thanks for inviting me, bro. It was intriguing."

Matthew said, "Intriguing? That is an understatement, professor," and lifted up one of the windshield wipers of his brother's car before bounding away into the night. William remained stoic despite his brother's annoying joke, but he had grown used to the teasing after thirty years of brotherhood. When William rolled down the window to fix his windshield wiper, though, he failed to notice the biting chill in the air and the shimmer of frost on the grass and pavement.

On the drive home, he kept revisiting the dialogue between Barker and the old professor and wondered how the family letter fit into reality. Though he enjoyed the intellectualisms of Barker, William still considered his conclusions to be human deification in the garb of science and progress—simply substituting man and technology for God and Spirit. Still, it made his head hurt to consider the ramifications of either believing or denying God and Jesus.

Perhaps it was why he didn't notice until too late that his car had begun to slide across the icy road toward the steep cliff leading to the river below.

Chapter Twelve

Baptism

In the morning, the guards pulled Alon, Naamah, Silas, and two others out of the jail and put them into another caged carriage. This time, though, they were unshackled and could move freely about the enclosure. When asked, the driver reluctantly admitted they were on their way north to Thessalonica and would arrive the next morning.

Alon knew enough of the area to know that the city of Thessalonica housed one of the bigger Roman arenas. He had hoped for imprisonment in a salt mine, but this meant he and his daughter—in fact, everyone in the caged carriage—were traveling to their deaths. He could accept that for himself, but he refused to entertain the thought for his daughter. She would be free. It could happen no other way. No matter what happened to him, she would survive.

The fellow prisoner named Silas moved next to him and said, "Hello, friend. I pray that you are faring well."

Alon almost laughed at the absurdness of the question. He replied, "God hates us."

Silas looked down at Naamah and said, "I understand why you might think that, brother, but God still cares and will rescue us from death. You just have to have faith in Him."

Alon moved Naamah off his lap and turned to Silas. "Listen— 'brother'—I followed God my whole life until Eldad and Barnabas introduced me to Yeshua. Since then, my wife died, Eldad was stoned, and my daughter and I were falsely arrested for public disturbance." Alon poked him in the chest. "If God is so great, then why are we here? I thought He loved us, but this is beyond cruelty."

Alon expected more, but Silas responded, "I am so sorry, brother. I don't always understand why God leads us through such rocky paths, but I have seen Him rescue His children time and time again from imprisonment and from illness."

"Yeah?" Alon replied. "Then, why isn't He freeing us now, Silas? Why?"

Silas lowered his head a bit, and Alon saw Silas's eyes well with tears. "I asked myself the same thing when the Jewish leaders in Antioch took my wife and had her flogged to death."

Silas's admission startled Alon.

"I was so filled with hate for those wicked people. All I wanted to do was kill them. And I was so disappointed in God, but then a fellow citizen named Saul of Tarsus—now called Paul—helped me understand the power of God through Jesus Christos."

"I. . . have heard of Paul, a Christian Roman citizen. Barnabas told me about him. You're a citizen, too? You met him?"

"Met him?" Silas replied, wiping his eyes. "I traveled with him for years. You cannot believe what I saw him do through the power of Yeshua—the blind could see, the lame could walk, the deaf could speak. But more than that, brother, Paul helped people see God, which not even death can take away. I even helped heal people with the power of the Holy Spirit—me! Who am I to do the work of the Lord?"

Feeling bad that he poked Silas in the chest so hard, Alon said, "That sounds familiar, Silas. Eldad spoke that way, but I still don't understand why we are here and why God has allowed my daughter to be arrested and set for execution."

"All we can do is pray, my friend. And I can tell you what Paul said to me one day. I helped him write it down in a letter to the church in Philippi. He said, 'To live is Christos and to die is gain. But if I am to live on in the flesh, this will mean fruitful labor for me; and I do not know which to choose. But I am hard-pressed from both directions, having the desire to depart and be with Christos, for that is very much better; yet to remain on in the flesh is more necessary for your sake.'"

"What does that mean, Silas?"

Silas put a comforting hand on Alon' shoulder and said, "It means, I know why you want to live—your daughter, Naamah—but you have to understand that there is more to life than just this existence. Paul told me about his encounter with the risen Yeshua. Even in Paul's overwhelming conviction and guilt over what he had done to the Lord's sheep, Paul felt the glorious, accepting, healing love of God. It was like nothing he had ever experienced before, and he often longed to return to that place again. He called it, 'Home.' Death is just the way home for us, brother, for those who have been baptized in Yeshua's name."

Silas noticed Alon looked away and asked, "Weren't you baptized by Barnabas or Eldad?"

Still looking away, Alon said, "No. . . I wasn't sure I was ready to commit. I was afraid it would get me in trouble." He looked at Silas and they both laughed.

Silas replied, "Apparently, God was ready for you, my brother."

"Not much we can do about that now, Silas."

Silas jumped to his feet and said, "Not necessarily, Alon. Hold on." He moved to the front of the caged carriage and spoke to the driver.

The driver pulled over to the side of the road and jumped down from the seat holding three sets of shackles in hand.

Alon turned to Silas and asked, "What did you say to him?"

Silas replied, "I reminded him that I have Roman citizenship, but more importantly, I told him that if he let me baptize you and Naamah, we'd all smell better upwind."

Naamah giggled when she heard Silas's explanation.

One of the other guards opened the door of the carriage and said, "All right, citizen, you have ten minutes. Put these on first."

Alon never saw anyone smile as they put on chains as Silas did, but he also slid them around his ankles and those of his daughter, and the three stepped out of the carriage. The other prisoners were sleeping and did not stir despite the noise. Once the door was closed and locked, they began to walk down an embankment with the guards close behind.

At the bottom, Alon noticed a modest stream, about six feet wide and maybe three feet deep at the most. Silas stepped into the stream and held out his hands to Alon.

"Are you ready, brother?"

Alon stumbled into the stream and stood beside Silas. "Yes, Silas. I am."

Silas said, "Then kneel, Alon."

With one hand behind his head and the other holding onto Alon's hands, Silas looked up to heaven and said, "Alon, I baptize you in the name of the Father, of his Son, Yeshua, and of the Holy Counselor who has called you by name."

Silas lowered Alon into the stream, and he felt the filth of the past days wash away. More than that, Alon felt a whole life of hurting God and others vanish in the living stream around him. Silas lifted him out again, saying, "The old self is washed away; Yeshua has cleansed you of all sins, my brother. Go with God."

The water dripping down his face couldn't hide the tears of joy from his eyes, and his heart filled with even more joy when he heard his daughter say, "My turn, Daddy! My turn!" which he and Silas obliged.

Walking back to the caged carriage, Alon said, "Thank you, Silas, for baptizing me and my daughter."

"Don't thank me, brother Alon. You weren't baptized in my name or Paul's or Barnabas's. You were baptized in Yeshua's name and brought here for some great work. I know it. I just know it."

Standing at the cage door, Alon looked at the soldiers, his daughter, Silas, and the prisoners inside and said, "I believe it now, Silas, and I know the good work is coming soon for all of us."

The guards closed the cage door and continued on their way to Thessalonica, the showground notorious for entertainment and executions.

Chapter Thirteen

Discovery

Aelia felt so good after Luke's visit that she insisted that Gaius take her on his next "training" excursion. He and Justus did their best to talk her out of the trip, but she wouldn't take no for an answer. They didn't fight her too long, concerned that an argument might bring back the disorder, but Aelia never worried about it again in her pregnancy.

Since Luke healed her from her bleeding illness and intense uterine pain, she felt like she could climb Mt. Vesuvius, and she knew that their child inside was stronger than it had ever been. Moreover, something inside her told her it was going to be a boy, which would make her husband and father very pleased indeed.

Both Gaius and Justus agreed that Aelia did need to get out of the villa for some rest and relaxation. The gods knew she had suffered enough in the months earlier to warrant it. They conspired to keep her unawares of Gaius's true work until the event itself. Hopefully, they could talk her into going shopping instead of viewing Gaius on the arena floor.

Since the physician's first visit and with each week's checkup, Aelia had begun to act differently than before in her relationship with Gaius and even her parents. Justus had attributed it to her becoming a mature woman. Gaius assumed it was because her humors were in perfect balance with the child. *This is why,* he told himself, *women should be pregnant all the time—it was good for their countenance* (and subsequently, household harmony).

They loaded up her father's cart with wine to sell at the market and Gaius's armor and weaponry. If covetous eyes wanted to steal the wine barrels from the couple, the trappings of a seasoned warrior kept them at bay. With his other daughters, Justus worried about them traveling about the countryside, but with Gaius alongside Aelia, Justus worried more about the countryside.

With some fond farewells and crocodile tears from her mother (and some from Aelia), the happy couple took off for their four-day journey along the well-constructed Roman road. It was a bumpy but uneventful trip for both of them, and they enjoyed each other's company and conversations. In a way, it made them feel like newlyweds again, off to discover the world, with excitement and hope in front of them.

When they arrived, they first checked into their lodgings, which happened to be owned by Gaius's cousin, Flavius, and his wife Julia. Aelia and Julia had become good friends long ago as children under the tutelage of the same Greek doctore—Timaeus, also known as the

Sophist. Gaius and Flavius were also the best of friends and more like brothers than cousins. Visits such as these were precious to both parties.

As the men were unpacking the cart, Julia came up and hugged Aelia and squeaked in delight. "Oh, this is going to be such an exciting vacation for you," Julia said.

"I don't know," Aelia replied. "I figure you and I can do some shopping in the center while Gaius trains the troops."

Julia locked arms with Aelia and walked her into the courtyard of their villa and said, "Is he training soldiers, too? I didn't think he would have the energy after his exploits as an *auctorati*."

Aelia's face grew red, and Julia realized she had unwittingly informed on Gaius.

"Oh, I am sorry, Aelia. I thought you knew. Gaius has been doing this for sometime. He told Flavius it was to pay for your medical treatments and medicine. I don't think he was trying to deceive you; I think he was protecting you from worrying when you were sicker."

Aelia knew that was the case, but it didn't make her feel better about Gaius being an *auctorati*. Besides the danger of it, she remembered attending the events in the arena and peeking when her father told her not to look at the people being executed. The *auctorati* not only battled each other, they also slaughtered the enemies of the state—some quickly, and some in cruel, drawn-out fashion. She hated to think of her husband that way.

Later that night, when Gaius returned from dropping off the wine and after dinner, Aelia confronted him about his involvement in the arena.

"You should have told me, Gaius," she blurted out.

Aware that she knew at last, Gaius responded, "I was worried you would worry too much, my sweet, and your father and I. . ."

"My father thinks I am a simple woman who should mind her place. You know better than that, my love."

Gaius put his arms around his wife and said, "I was afraid of doing anything else that would cause me to lose you or the baby. I already messed up with the trip to your parents' villa. I couldn't make another mistake."

"But you think fighting and killing in the arena is not a mistake? What if you were killed or maimed? Do you want your child to grow up fatherless? We need you, Gaius. You can't do this again."

Gaius stepped back from Aelia and held her at arm's length, saying, "This will be the last time, my love. I promise. The physician's fees are not as exorbitant as Menander's, but the medicine they have you on is not cheap. One more battle in the arena should buy enough to last you through the next two months. Then I am done."

Looking into his eyes, Aelia asked, "Will you kill Christians in the arena, Gaius?"

Gaius released her and moved over to an adjacent table, picked up the pitcher, and watched the red wine pour into the brass goblet. "Maybe. I am not the procurator or governor, Aelia." Still looking down at his wine, he said, "I am just a simple soldier who does what he is told."

Aelia walked to Gaius and put her hand on his back. "You know that Luke is a Christian, Gaius."

"Yes," he replied.

"You know that he prayed to God for our baby, and we were healed."

Gaius drained the glass of wine. "To which god did he pray, Aelia— Zeus? Apollo? Athena? Asclepis? I don't put much stock in what the religious zealots spout. Nor should you, being the quintessential cynic."

Aelia turned Gaius around and looked him in the eyes and said, "Gaius, all I know is that I was in incredible torment and pain. Menander didn't help me. The medicine didn't help me. Our baby was dying. Then this physician from Philippi came and spoke to his god for me—for all of us—and now our baby lives. This is a gift from God. You shouldn't ignore it, my love."

Gaius took Aelia's hands and held them close to his heart. "What would you have me do, Aelia? I have sold myself for one more exhibition. If I back out, then the money must be returned, or they will throw me into jail until it is returned. And we have no money unless I do this."

She rested her head against his chest. "I don't know, Gaius. Just follow your heart tomorrow and consider your actions. You are a good man— that's why I married you. But good men protect those who are weak. They don't murder people who cannot defend themselves."

"I. . . I. . . will try, my love," Gaius promised without much assurance in his tone.

"Perhaps we can pray to Luke's God—the God—and seek for deliverance for you all," Aelia asked.

"I have no bird or goat to sacrifice, Aelia," Gaius responded.

"Luke taught me that you don't need a sacrifice with this God. He already paid the price for us all."

"What?" Gaius replied, shaking his head. "What will satisfy this God then? How can we bribe him?"

"Just have the belief that He can help us, Luke said, and this God is pleased."

Gaius scratched his head and said, "Well, I think I might be able to afford that, my love."

Aelia smiled and led Gaius by the hand out into the courtyard lit up by the blue light of the crescent moon. Sitting on a bench and staring up at the stars above, she taught Gaius the prayer she heard Luke speak the night God had healed their child.

Together, they prayed for wisdom, they prayed for healing, and they prayed for deliverance—simple, rough, unsophisticated prayers from expectant yet tangled hearts trying to make sense of love and life. And yet, deep inside, Aelia felt she could count on this God above all gods to help them again.

Gaius, on the other hand, didn't know what to think or say or hope from this new Yeshua god. His life of soldiering, which used to be so clear in his mind, now seemed foreign, as he felt the baby kick within his beloved wife. Life had become precious. Could he now kill without offending this god? A conscience is the most dangerous of liabilities in the arena. The faith of his wife, though, was convicting. He wanted to write it off as a "maternal madness," as her father called it, but Gaius couldn't help but see the truth and goodness in what Aelia and Luke suggested.

Staring up at the night sky, Aelia rested in his arms, and he decided to take a chance. Gaius offered a silent prayer of his own to this Yeshua. "Okay, then, if you exist and you do not want me to kill anymore, then make a way, God of all gods. I have no choice if I want to stay alive or out of prison. So, make it right. And if you do, I promise that I will believe." This was the simple but direct prayer of a soldier, and it was the best he could do. He hoped it was enough.

Chapter Fourteen

Hand of God

William hadn't been traveling very fast when his car went off the road—just forty miles per hour—but with the ice on the road in front of the bridge, and going downhill, he might as well have been going seventy for the lack of control over the car. In a desperate attempt to correct the direction it was moving, William spun the steering wheel sharp to the right, but all that managed to do was to rotate his car ninety degrees, so that it went off the road parallel to it rather than perpendicular.

When the car hit the side of the road, William yelled out, "Jeeeeeesussss!" and it flipped over into the darkness. William tried to scream again, but despite being seat-belted, his head slammed onto the dashboard, which had been pushed toward him two feet when the car smashed onto one of the boulders down the precipice. Woozy from his head wound, he felt himself being turned over and over again in the car, with jarring blows from the surrounding trees and boulders striking him and his metal cushion. It seemed to go on forever, but the car finally stopped, with its front end facing up toward the road.

Through blurry, bloody eyes, William could make out the lights of the bridge above him, and he could hear the roaring of the river below the car. He tried to make sense of what had just happened, but his body had begun to go into shock, and he lay there, like an astronaut ready for liftoff, unable to move.

A loud metallic snap, followed by a high-pitched ping, woke him up enough to realize that the car wasn't done moving yet. He could feel it inching down the hillside, but then he understood enough to recognize that the car was hanging from the cliff, dangling over the cold winter water below. He had to get out fast before the car plunged into the river.

Despite the sheer terror of the moment, he tried not to rush his movements, lest his actions cause the car to go over quicker than it already was. He tried to release his seat belt, but it had jammed, of course, and he couldn't unlock it. Fortunately for him, on the way down the embankment, the thrashing of his body had loosed the belt somewhat, and there was enough slack to wiggle out. He was just trying to decide whether to wiggle underneath it or over it without rocking the car.

He slid the diagonal strap over his throbbing head, and, pushing his knees against the dashboard and using his elbows on the top of the car seat, began to liberate himself from the belt. He had all but one leg free when the rock holding the car above the water shattered under the weight. For a moment, he felt like he was weightless in space, but he knew that sensation was short-lived.

Sure enough, the car dropped twenty feet and hit the water below as if William had rammed a brick wall at forty miles per hour. The force threw him into the backseat, and the water gushed in from seemingly everywhere. William tried to open the back doors, but in his fear, forgot he had to first unlock them before the handles would work.

Within a half a minute, the cab of the car filled up with icy, numbing water, and William managed a breath before going under. He pounded against the side windows with his arms and kicked with all his might, but the water pressure hindered his efforts. He knew he couldn't hold his breath much longer, but he managed to move back to the front of the car in hopes that those doors would open. They did not. The blows of the boulders and trees had crushed and sealed the doors to the car frame as it rolled down the ravine.

William beat again against the side windows and the windshield, but his movements grew slower and weaker with each passing second. When the final supply of oxygen in his lungs was used up, he realized that his questions about God were about to be answered. Too weak to struggle, he let the blackness envelope his body and waited for death to come.

The darkness exploded away when the brightest light that William had ever seen shot into the cab, illuminating everything in a shimmering golden hue. It was as if the beams from every sunrise and sunset had combined within the cab around him. It was then that William saw what looked like a giant hand, about three feet across the knuckles, punch in the windshield and then toss it aside like napkin. The hand then moved into the cab and cradled William's body, pulling him out of the doomed vehicle. The hand was warm and soft but fleshy, and, for some reason, it brought back a childhood memory of being bathed in the kitchen sink by his mother—the soapy water—warm and soothing, sweet caring eyes looking down upon him, and comforting sounds telling him all would be all right. William could not help but close his eyes and slip away into unconsciousness.

He awoke faceup on the rocks beside the river, with sirens and firemen belaying down the cliff to get to him. His head pounded like it would explode. His legs and arms ached from the coldness. He looked around for the giant hand and thought for a moment that he saw the golden glimmer inside his car as it slipped to the bottom of the deep river, but his eyes were blurry from his head wound.

The rescuers were soon by his side. With all the noise of the river and sirens, he could barely hear the fireman tell him he was going to be fine and he was going to make it. He began to laugh and cry at the same time. After they rolled him into the backboard lift and secured him in, William felt at peace despite the acute pain all over his body. In his heart, he knew that his rescue was more than just being pulled from a dying car or frigid river. Something beyond the realm of nature and normal reality had saved him—his life attested to it—and he found the earlier proclamations of anti-theist Mr. Barker to be less credible and brilliant. William now had personal knowledge, personal empirical data, that confirmed life beyond the normal perspective. How else could he explain what happened?

Despite his injuries, he felt a newfound sense of direction, a sense of comfort and joy he had never experienced before, and it made him almost thankful for the car wreck. The seeming insanity of thankfulness in time of catastrophe brought the letter to mind, and when he returned home six hours later, his arm in a cast, a bandage covering the twenty-five stitches across his right temple, and without the approval of his neurologist who wanted him to stay overnight for observation, William sat down in his favorite leather smoking chair, Claudius curled up at his feet, and he began reading the last chapter of the letter.

Chapter Fifteen

The Arena

> *"We write unto you, brethren, an account of what befell those that suffered martyrdom and especially the blessed Polycarp, who stayed the persecution, having as it were set his seal upon it by his martyrdom. For nearly all the foregoing events came to pass that the Lord might show us once more an example of martyrdom which is conformable to the Gospel."* ~ *Polycarp 1:1*

All the condemned in the dark moldy holding cell—both men and women—could hear the shouts and savage roar of the Romans in the amphitheater above them.

Alon sat next to his daughter, Naamah, and held her close, trying to provide some fleeting comfort to her in the few minutes they had left before their turns in the arena. Her little body shook as she wept, and when she did stop every so often, he heard her whisper a soft, desperate prayer for mommy to take her home. Though he felt some peace since their impromptu baptism in the river, he hoped Naamah's prayer came true—that God was listening, and that this was just a painful chapter they had to go through before release from all worries and torment. Still, his heart ached in sorrow for his daughter, and he wondered why people could be so cruel.

A loud thump startled them as bodies crashed above them, tossing dirt down the cracks of their holding cell roof, and they all looked up when they heard the crowd roar in horrible excitement with the screams of the man being executed. "Animals!" spat Sakarbaal, one of the men in the cell with them. "What sort of people are these Romans?"

Silas was among them, and he put his hand on Sakarbaal's shoulder and spoke to him with calmed assurance. "Remember what Yeshua said. 'They know not what they do.' This is even more true today, my son."

Sakarbaal shook off the comforting hand. "I know not of your god, Christ-lover. As far as I am concerned, you're slightly better than them," he replied pointing upwards. "But they're monsters, old man. Monsters." More bloodthirsty cheers from the stadium above seemed to prove his case.

Her voice breaking with emotion, another woman, Elissa, reached out to take hold of Sakarbaal's hand. "Not monsters, brother. They are full of anger and pain, which blinds them."

Her words seemed to agitate him more. "Yet they are free, and we are soon to die, sister. And no foolish prayers to some foreign god will change that."

Releasing his hand, her head sunk low and she replied, "Perhaps not, but we will soon see Baal, and they will be stuck in this hellhole. What reward do they get? Nothing but blood and sadness." Sakarbaal reached out his hand to his sister and pulled her close. She wept into his shoulder.

The condemned hearts began to beat wildly when the Roman guard banged on the cell door and shouted, "Prepare yourselves, prisoners! You're up next." With the guard's proclamation, Sakarbaal slumped into the bench and covered his head with his hands. "Oh, Baal! Why's this happening?" he pleaded aloud.

Silas stood up slowly, but with purpose, and walked to the center of the holding cell. "My family, brother Paul said that men would persecute us because of our hope, for they covet what they do not have and they wish to destroy our joy with God whom they hate. You are here and I regret that, but we have a choice of how we live and how we die. I, for one, am going to die well for God."

"What does that mean, old man?" Sakarbaal snarled, tears streaming down his dirty cheeks.

Silas walked over one of the older men in the cell and helped him to his feet. He turned and did likewise to Alon and Naamah. "It means ending my days with a heart of love for you. . . and them. . . because I can. Because of Yeshua." Looking deep into Alon's eyes, he said,

"And you can, too, my brother. Don't let the darkness win. Fight it with your last breath."

Alon wiped the tears away and said, "I will, Silas. I will." The three embraced.

"I plan on fighting the Romans with all I have, Christ-lover," Sakarbaal interjected.

Silas turned to him and said, "Then you will gain the rewards of violence and hatred, my son."

"You waste my last time with words of peace for the wicked Roman mob. They are all bastards deserving death. Hannibal stopped too soon. We should have crushed them."

Recognizing that time indeed was short, most of the cellmates held hands in a tight group as Silas began to pray for them. Naamah held out her hand to Elissa, who took it, and joined the group. Sakarbaal began to object, but then the wooden doors of the cell were kicked open, enveloping them in a blazing bright light. And the crowd screamed at them to come forth for their murderous amusement.

Alon held Naamah's hand and spoke above the noise, "God have mercy," as they were pushed out into the hot dusty center of the coliseum.

The scene surrounding them was a nightmare to behold. Twenty or so men were hanging on crosses set up on the edge of the arena floor, screaming and writhing in pain. Alon looked down and saw blood pools and body parts strewn everywhere, along with giant lion tracks, he assumed. In front of each of the crucified men stood a mighty gladiator, growling and shouting at the prisoners, save for Gaius, who stood in quiet dread of the impending event, his mask hiding his torment.

Alon's Latin was not very good, but he knew enough to get the gist of the gladiators' taunts and threats. The gladiator nearest to them, Gallus, called out to Alon and Naamah and swore they would be the first ones he would kill for Jupiter's glory. Alon knelt down in front of his daughter and held her close, speaking loud enough for her to hear over the bloodthirsty crowd.

"Naamah, we are finally going to see mommy."

Naamah looked up with tearful and perceptive eyes. "I know, Daddy. I have missed her so much."

Alon hugged her tight and said, "Me, too, sweetheart. Me, too. Remember that whatever happens, I love you so much. I can't wait to be with you in heaven."

Naamah put both of her little dirty hands on his cheeks and said, "It'll be okay, Daddy. We were baptized. That means we have a home with God."

Choking back his sobs, Alon replied, "That's right, baby. We're going home."

The governor of Thessalonica stood up and motioned to the trumpeters who let loose a blast from their instruments. The crowd cheered. It was time.

True to his word, Gallus charged toward Alon and Naamah, shoving several shrieking prisoners to the ground. His sole intent in executing the wicked father and daughter was their being part of the pernicious cult upsetting the *Pax Romana* all over the empire.

Alon saw him coming. He then pulled Naamah's head into his shoulder and said to his daughter, "Close your eyes, Naamah, and don't open them for anything." She obeyed her father without question.

Gallus jumped in front of them with a loud yell and raised his sword to strike his first blow. Alon stared into the gladiator's eyes and saw darkness and hatred. He was surprised, because instead of feeling contempt or fear from this menacing Roman, Alon felt pity and love. He wondered why the man hated them so much.

Gallus intended to behead them both with one motion, which he hoped would impress the governor and the director of the arena. With Gaius in the arena with him, he knew he had competition, which meant a smaller portion of the winnings at the end if he didn't amaze the crowd. He was going to make this man and child's execution a bloody, disgusting show sure to bring him notice, but he didn't see one of the prisoners racing toward him, with hateful and violent eyes of his own, approaching from the rear.

Sakarbaal launched into the air and snapped Gallus's neck when his feet collided with the back of the gladiator's head. Alon just stood there, holding Naamah, in shock as the body of Gallus flopped down in front of them like one of his daughter's old rag dolls. Sakarbaal picked up the sword and yelled at Alon, "Get up, Christian, and help me destroy these bastards!"

Silas ran toward the three prisoners, calling out, "Put down the sword, brother! Put down the sword! He who lives by the sword. . ." but he never finished his warning because another one of the other gladiators thrust his spear into Silas's side, piercing his heart. Dying instantly, Silas dropped like a stone to the arena floor. The crowd screamed even louder.

Gaius hadn't joined in the fighting, but when he saw Sakarbaal kill Gallus, his military instincts took over, and he began to stalk this new threat, sinking low to the ground like a cat hunting its prey. From the arena seats, Aelia saw her husband move in for the kill, and prayed to God, "Yeshua, please help him. Keep him from destroying himself. Please, God. Please. . ."

Alon and Naamah stood between Gaius and Sakarbaal, but Gaius paused a moment in front of the pair. His first thought was that he could execute them easily, but, as he looked at father and daughter trying to stay alive, he couldn't help but wonder what he would be thinking were it him and his child in this arena of terror. All he did was nod to them before running around them toward Sakarbaal.

Alon was taken aback. *Mercy? From a Roman gladiator? God must have spoken to the man's heart,* he reasoned. Perhaps there was hope for them after all.

Sakarbaal managed to dispatch another one of the younger, inexperienced gladiators by running around him and delivering smaller blows between the Roman's armor. When the gladiator grew faint with blood loss, Sakarbaal kicked his legs out from under him and plunged the sword into his belly. The young gladiator screamed in pain, and the audience screamed in anger for revenge.

Gaius tried to be silent as he approached Sakarbaal, but he kicked a loose helmet on the ground into a fallen shield and the clang gave Sakarbaal notice of his intentions. He turned and faced Gaius, unafraid and unconcerned for his own welfare. Sakarbaal knew this would end in his death, so why not take as many out as possible? He didn't believe in Hades, Olympus, or heaven, or whatever trendy deity his sister pleaded with him to follow. He just believed in himself, his ability, and his sword.

The two circled each other, trying to ascertain the other's weakness, and the crowd began to "boo" them when the fight remained stagnant. Sakarbaal lunged first and their swords crashed together, showering the ground with sparks. Sakarbaal was stronger than Gaius had anticipated, and the blow pushed him back a bit, which Sakarbaal perceived. This made him pursue Gaius with more ferocity. Soon, Gaius found himself in defensive mode, deflecting and parrying Sakarbaal's sword, which crept closer and closer to tender flesh.

Gaius tried to keep his focus on his enemy, but in the back of his mind, he couldn't forget his prayer with Aelia in the garden and his promise to Yeshua. In a moment of foolishness, he looked up into the stands where he knew where Aelia was sitting, and that second was all Sakarbaal needed to deliver a slicing blow into Gaius side below his chest plate. He screamed in pain, and Sakarbaal sidearmed him, sending Gaius flying to the ground. He tried to lift up his sword in protection, but Sakarbaal just kicked it away, laughing.

Alon had picked up Naamah and was moving between the fighters, trying to stay in peaceful territory. When he saw Sakarbaal towering above the gladiator who helped them earlier, he set Naamah down and ran to his fellow prisoner and yelled, "Sakarbaal! Don't do it. He's not a bad man."

Sakarbaal pressed his sword to Gaius's throat and said, "Here that, Roman dog? You're not a bad man."

"No," Gaius responded. "You are wrong, prisoner. I am not a good man."

Sakarbaal looked down for a moment and then pulled his sword up six inches to plunge into Gaius's neck. From behind, both men heard Alon say, "Don't do it, brothers. There is nothing gained from killing each other. Only a second death later on." Alon held out his hand to Sakarbaal. "Give me the sword. Don't let the darkness win, friend."

Sakarbaal relented for a moment, but then he saw Elissa from behind Alon get struck in the face by one of the remaining gladiators, and he hissed at Alon. "You want it, Christian? Here you go," and he plunged his sword into Alon' stomach.

Alon sank to the ground but grabbed the sword, and, with his remaining strength, he wouldn't let go. "No, brother. No more killing," Alon said to him. Sakarbaal tried to wrestle the sword free, but by the time he finally sliced off Alon's fingers and freed the blade, another gladiator with a huge battle-axe swung and struck him across the chest, catapulting him backwards ten feet to his death.

Naamah cried out, "Daddy!" and ran to his side, crying. She tried to stop the blood pouring out from her father's wound, but it was too much for such little hands. The axe-wielding gladiator raised his weapon to finish them both off, but stopped mid-lunge when Gaius called out, "Nerva, halt! These are mine." Gaius got to his feet, and the junior gladiator, though much taller and stronger, submitted to the authority of the famous Corinthian *auctorati*.

The noise from the crowd was deafening. This had been more carnage and thrills than they had ever expected. There would be much celebrating in the city tonight, but two prisoners remained, and their fate was undecided.

The governor arose once again and held out his hands to silence the crowd. They quieted down in seconds. Gaius picked up his sword, stood over Alon and his weeping daughter, Naamah, and called out to the ruler, "Mercy? Yes?" The crowd screamed out, "Noooooo!" They wanted more carnage, but Gaius wanted to save these two at all costs. He wondered how far he would have to go to do that.

The governor held out his right hand, thumb extended. The crowd cried out, "*Volumus sanguine! Volumus sanguine! O, magnus regem.*" The politician smiled as he looked around, and then with a quick motion, pulled his thumb across his neck, left to right, indicating execution for the two—no mercy.

Gaius's heart sank. He had no choice. If he didn't kill them, then Nerva would be ordered to kill them and then him. If he died, who would take care of Aelia and his son? Somehow, he knew that their child was a boy. He knelt down beside Alon and whispered in his ear, "I promise that I will make it quick and painless, brother."

Alon smiled at his merciful executioner and gasped out, "I know. . . I. . . forgive you. . ."

Alon pulled Naamah on top of him and said, "Together. . . please." Understanding, Gaius nodded and stood up, sword in hand. One single blow for both through the heart—instant death for this man and his beloved child.

Holding the hilt toward the sky, Gaius raised his sword, blade down, tears cutting lines in his dirty and bloody face. He was filled with sorrow and disgrace for his life and legacy of killing and suffering. All he could say was, "Please, God," as he started to bring the sword downwards.

A sound like thunder exploded inside the arena, and, in a millisecond, the ground beneath Gaius, Nerva, Alon, and Naamah heaved up like a great wave crashing into the rocks, throwing them apart.

The arena itself looked as if God was taking his finger and stirring it around and around, mixing the scene with granite blocks, wooden timbers, and screaming spectators. The quake lasted for almost three minutes—an eternity when one is in the midst of the earthly chastisement. When the rumbling and shaking ceased, all that could be heard was the weeping and wailing of men and women crushed and bleeding in need of rescue.

The governor's box was hit the hardest when the pillars holding up the triangular portico slid out, and the marble slab fell upon the highest of Roman society and government, crushing them and their future plans. Somehow, the governor managed to escape being killed, but his wife and one of his daughters did not fair as fortunate. He was sitting on one of the columns, shaking and gibbering, the remaining attendants wiping the blood from his head and asking, "What should we do? What should we do, now?"

Gaius straightway looked up to the stands, afraid of what he would see. Instead, he saw his wife dusty and coughing, waving at him, indicating that she and their cousins were okay. He looked and saw Naamah sitting on the ground, her father's head in her lap. He walked over to them. Alon was dead.

Gaius sank to his knees in front of the pair and reached out to hold Alon's hand. He wept. He couldn't bear to look at the little girl but said, "I am so sorry, child."

Naamah brushed the hair from her father's face and said, "Daddy's with mommy now."

Gaius nodded his head. "Yes, child, they are together."

Naamah pointed to the entrance of the arena and said, "During the earthquake, I saw them walking away. They waved to me and were smiling."

Gaius looked at Naamah to see her face but could only say, "Uh. . . I don't. . ."

"Daddy said not to worry about them. They are happy with God. But he said that I was supposed to find someone named. . . Gaius? Do you know him?" She looked up at him with innocent trusting eyes.

Gaius stared at her for a moment, his hand over his mouth, but admitted to her, "I. . . am Gaius."

Naamah just said, "Oh!" and bent down and kissed her father on the cheek. She laid his head on the ground as she slid out and stood up, walked to Gaius, and took his hand.

"Time to go home," she said.

Amazed at the wonder of this little girl holding his hand, he replied, "Yes, let's go home, my child," and the two walked together to meet Aelia to travel to a new life together—a gift from God.

Gaius remembered his prayer and promise to God. He had no trouble speaking in the years to come of how one miraculous healing of a leper led to the redemption of a murderous gladiator and the powerful impact of an astounding, unimagined, orphaned daughter of God.

Conclusion

Williiam turned to the last page of the letter, halfway expecting it to open up into a hallway of heaven like some icon hanging in an ancient Irish church, but instead, he found another letter from his great-grandfather, Alexander J. Berrit.

"Dear Son or Daughter of Most High,

As God is my witness (and may He forgive me for swearing to Him), the aforementioned epistle is true and faithful. Much like the well-known physician, I also have examined this text and tested its veracity without disappointment, I might add, as have my fathers and forefathers.

Specifically, I know that my great-grandfather, Cecil T. Berrit, travelled to Florence, Italy, in 1735, and found collaboration in the papal library (much thanks to the gracious permission of Cardinal Barberini) in the lives of the family martyrs and saints beginning with Alon in the first century, through the Age of Constantine, Gregory the Great, the Vikings, the

Renaissance, the Reformers, until today, praise His great and awesome name.

I was informed that a second family letter does exist (and possibly others), but that Cecil Berrit left it in the capable hands of Barberini for assistance with its translation. Unfortunately, Cecil received the pox and died before retrieving it from the good cardinal. Perhaps if one is quickened by the Lord, the reader will dare venture to the continent and discover more of the Berrit story of faith. From my father, I hear the second letter contains remarkable stories of conviction and the miracles of God's embrace of those who followed after Alon.

Again, may God open your eyes to the great sacrifice and devotion of your ancestors described within, who, through great love and devotion, fought the good fight and brought the blessings of God to all generations of his humble servants.

God bless and keep you all until His glorious return.

With the utmost of Sincerity and Hope,
Alexander J. Berrit, DD
December 25, 1856

William closed the book and took in a deep breath, pondering the letter and his miraculous escape in the river. Grabbing his laptop, he opened it and began to compose an e-mail to his brother, but stopped because he had no idea what to say to him. He kept the message short, saying he had been in an accident but he was well, although they needed to talk about life and God. He hit "SEND" and closed his eyes.

He thought about the letter: how it told the story of one man who, two thousand years ago, healed the lives of those around him, and how the golden thread of His love and true life spread from one person to another and another in an increasing tapestry of godliness and goodness.

Everyone is a on a journey—Eldad, Alon, Naamah, Gaius, Aelia, Matthew, William—and all will encounter pain and uncertainty. We can run away from God into the darkness and emptiness of the world, or we can courageously walk hand-in-hand with Him, knowing that walking in the light is the way to find true fulfillment and treasure beyond comparison. It all begins with belief and hope.

William opened his eyes, patted Claudius on the head, and said, "I believe." He then took out his laptop and checked on flights to Florence, Italy, during the summer hiatus.

THE END

Afterword

The Christian life has never been an easy one. In fact, I am not sure the Disciples really understood what the future would hold for them when Jesus said,

These things I have spoken to you so that you may be kept from stumbling. They will make you outcasts from the synagogue, but an hour is coming for everyone who kills you to think that he is offering service to God. These things they will do because they have not known the Father or Me. But these things I have spoken to you, so that when their hour comes, you may remember that I told you of them. These things I did not say to you at the beginning, because I was with you. (John 16).

And the Messiah was true to His words, and, as this story has offered, good people suffered for the Good News, but good still came from their pain and deaths.

Every Christian has a salvation story stretching back to the first century AD. Every Christian has an ancient sponsor who heard the news of Jesus Christ and embraced the message of the Holy Spirit, becoming brothers and sisters in Christ, joyfully joining the eternal family of God. Yes, we make the choice, but others still influence and gracefully share the truth that stands above and against what society foolishly says is right. It is true now; it was true one hundred years ago, a thousand years ago, back to the origin of the faith. And the faith will continue to spread, even in the darkness of worldliness, until God's appointed time comes for the rescue of believers and for the judgment of the wicked.

Roman society was an immoral mess when Christ arrived. I have often wondered if the days of Noah were equally bad; perhaps Christ will come again when, as Micah states,

> *The godly person has perished from the land, And there is no upright person among men. All of them lie in wait for bloodshed; Each of them hunts the other with a net.*

> *Concerning evil, both hands do it well. The prince asks, also the judge, for a bribe, And a great man speaks the desire of his soul; So they weave it together. The best of them is like a briar, The most upright like a thorn hedge. The day when you post your watchmen, Your punishment will come. Then their confusion will occur. . . But as for me, I will watch expectantly for the Lord; I will wait for the God of my salvation. My God will hear me. Do not rejoice over me, O my enemy. Though I fall I will rise; Though I dwell in darkness, the Lord is a light for me (Micah 7).*

The thwarted kingship of Julius Caesar, assassinated in 44 BC by members of his own senate, had morphed into the embraced emperorship of Augustus, Tiberius, Caligula, Claudius, and Nero. These men dominated Roman culture, and through their deeds and actions, they set Rome on a course for opulence, decadence, and bloodshed. The *Pax Romana*, the Roman Peace, was built on the backs of conquered nations, oppressed people, avaricious leaders, and unspeakable immorality—all for the glory of Rome and the hedonism of the mob.

Such was the cultural milieu encountered by the first Christians. For whatever reason, though not a perpetual state of persecution, if Roman control of any territory was threatened by civil unrest, Rome was eager and willing to ruthlessly put a stop to the uprising. Often, it didn't matter who started it; being all about control and order, the "troublesome" elements of society were removed publicly and coldly as a warning to all people considering challenging Roman hegemony.

There were three main periods of Roman persecution of the Christians: Emperor Nero to Emperor Domitian (AD 64–95), around the time of Emperor Trajan Decius (AD 112–250), and from Emperor Valerian to Emperor Diocletian (AD 250–311). Which emperor was the worst is probably unknown; all were feared and disliked by Christians and citizens alike. What is known is that the Christians became the targets of social scapegoating for all the problems of Roman society.

Christians were a small, eastern sect; they had not built up political friendships as some of the other minority groups in Rome had done. Thus, when others (such as the Herodian Jews) enjoyed favored emperor protection, the Christians quickly became easy objects of murderous entertainment for the Romans. Jesus had been truthful in his warnings.

All too often, Christian men, women, and children (of all ages) were thrown to the lions in the arenas, impaled on pikes or spears, drawn and quartered, killed by gladiators, and crucified and set on fire to light the arenas so that executions and festivities could go on despite the darkness (or more likely because of it). The Disciples and Apostles were the first to suffer and die at the hands of vicious, ungodly men; the church fathers (and mothers) soon followed, all for their strange beliefs that the Romans considered to be an evil "pernicious superstition," according to ancient Roman historian Tacitus (AD 56–117).

It was possible for the early believers to potentially avoid persecution and death for their "crimes." All they need do was to renounce Christ and give obedience to Caesar as Lord. The Cult of Emperor had nothing to do with religion and everything to do with politics. Unfortunately, Christianity, at that time, wanted nothing to do with politics and everything to do with deep personal faith in Jesus Christ, the Son of God and Savior of the world.

Though some Christians lapsed, many thousands did not disown their king and thus bravely died for their faith—Barnabas, Silas, Ignatius, Polycarp, Perpetua, and Felicity (to name but a few of these saints)—leaving a legacy and testimony not only to their fellow Christian brothers and sisters, but also to the whole of the Roman Empire.

In the darkness of their society—where humanity had turned righteousness and truthfulness on its head, and where the fruits of that system only demonstrated anger, violence, selfish pursuits, perversions of the flesh, and hardness of heart—these first Christians demonstrated the light of Christ in their daily lives through their piety, kindness, and morality, and even more so in their quiet, loving acceptance of martyrdom for Jesus.

The Christians had no worldly power, yet with Christ, they were stronger than the mightiest emperor. With Christ, they were not defeated; they were victorious. As Saint Paul encouraged them,

> *Only conduct yourselves in a manner worthy of the gospel of Christ, so that whether I come and see you or remain absent, I will hear of you that you are standing firm in one spirit, with one mind striving together for the faith of the gospel; in no way alarmed by your opponents—which is a sign of destruction for them, but of salvation for you, and that too, from God. For to you it has been granted for Christ's sake, not only to believe in Him, but also to suffer for His sake. . . (Philippians 1).*

Christianity has undergone a great deal of change culturally in the last two thousand years, and especially in the last fifty years. In my Church History classes, I often ask, "What would Peter, Paul, James, and John think of modern-day Christianity? Would they be ashamed or proud of our actions and deeds? Would they be affirming of the tenets and ethical manipulations of the 'New Christianity' promoted in the modern arena of the media or would they consider it *skubala*, as Paul puts it in the Epistle to the Philippians?

Contrary to what some intellectuals and scholars suggest, the first-century Christians believed in the Bible, felt deep appreciation and devotion to their Savior, and showed great hope and trust in God to take care of them in the present and beyond. Christ wasn't a metaphorical or figurative healer; He wasn't just a good teacher or ethical model to follow in life. Based on mountains and mountains of ancient religious documents, people believed in Jesus as the Son of God, and their lives were transformed.

Wonderfully, graciously, easily, the same still holds true for humanity today. As the Apostle John proclaims, *"All things came into being through Him, and apart from Him nothing came into being that has come into being. In Him was life, and the life was the Light of men" (John 1).*

If you are confused, if you are afraid, if you find yourself in the depths of despair, the first followers of Jesus would say, turn to God, turn to Jesus, and He will surely light your path to salvation.

Glossary

Abba = daddy, father (Greek)

Abortio = miscarriage (Latin)

Aelia = light, Sunlight (Latin)

Alon = oak tree (Hebrew)

Apollo = Roman god of light (Latin)

Asclepius = Roman god of medicine and healing (Greek)

Atropos = A goddess and daughter of Zeus who cut the life strings of all living beings (spun by her sister and fellow goddess, Clotho) when their final time of existence had been determined by Lachesis, another sister and fellow goddess.

Auctorati = volunteer gladiator

Ahuvi = sweetie (Hebrew)

Baal = ancient Phoenician and Canaanite fertility god (Carthage)

Beriyt = covenant (Hebrew)

Bibliotheca = library (Greek/Latin)

Carl Sagan = American astronomer, astrophysicist, author (d. 1996 CE)

Christos = Christ (Greek)

Cicero = Roman philosopher and statesman (d. 43 BCE)

Doctore = teacher (Latin)

Ecclesia = church or assembly (Greek)

Gaius = to rejoice (Latin)

Gallus = rooster (Latin)

Helios = the Greek god of the Sun

In statione = on guard (Latin)

John Lennox = Irish apologist. mathematician. and philosopher of science at Oxford.

Justus = justice (Latin)

Lanista (ae) = owner/trainer of gladiators

Libellus (Libelli) = Certificate of worship in the Cult of the Emperor

Magnus regem = great king

Mars = Roman god of war

Meira = enlightened (Hebrew)

Menander (and wife Phoebe) = Ephesian physician in first century CE

Muris = mouse (Latin)

Naamah = pleasant (Hebrew)

Nerva = strength (Latin)

Pater = father, daddy

Pharmacopola = pharmacist (Latin)

Pax Romana = period of stability in Roman Empire (27 BCE to 180 CE)

Pompeii Spectacula = ancient amphitheater in Pompeii, Italy

Primus = first

Principate = rule of the early Roman emperors

Puella = girl (Latin)

Sakarbaal = Ba'al remembered

Skubala = Dung or garbage

Thessalonica = Macedonian site of Roman arena used for gladiatorial combat in the first century.

Timaeus = also known as the Sophist (first to fourth century AD)

Vincere = I conquered (Latin)

Volumus sanguine = We want blood (Latin).

Y2K = 2000 CE, suggested by some to create global economic havoc, computer-wise

Zkenah = old woman

Ze'ev = wolf (Hebrew)